To Damian, Amanda, and Allyson

I love you!

CHAPTER ONE

I can sit here and try to tell you that everything goes as you plan it out to be, or I can sit here and tell you that the world is just one big messed up place. At least, to me it is just one big ball of mess. I could not even argue with you on the points that can prove to you that what I am saying is the truth. I will try to convince you that my points are right and whatever you thought just for one moment is all wrong, even though the evidence is right in front of you. Yet you are blinded by stupidity along with whatever you hear, you think is the absolute truth, but I am here to tell you that you are wrong.

I have witnessed firsthand that the world is not full of flowers and sweet lullabies. Demons are actually real and everyone is lying to themselves. Trying to forget reality, when the reality is right there screaming in their face, but I actually think that the reality is controlled by the Government. They decide what they want you to see and hear, it has been that way for years. The saddest part is that no one is going to question it, no one ever has. If there is even one squeal of rebellion, you automatically get sent to the nearest prison. Your name is never brought up again at that point. I have lost a few family members because of this.

The year is 2035, the United States is no longer the United States anymore. I mean that there are no longer any states due to the years of pollution that have plagued many generations before me. The Government found it necessary to build a Dome that takes up at least three states at and to put everyone into one nation under the same roof. They control everything that we do, from where we sleep to what we put in our mouths. They even control the times that we eat and sleep. We as a people are no longer allowed to think for ourselves. Not only do we have a chip inserted at birth, but we are also tattooed with a barcode and a number. Therefore I guess you can say that Dave is no longer called Dave, he is number 6825586156, Even though to me, He will still be Dave.

The Government even controls what we have in our home. They pick out the furniture that they force us to use. Microphones and cameras are also placed in the homes, you cannot even get naked in front of your own mirror in the bathroom without the Government knowing. Children and teens are not allowed to put posters up in their bedrooms because it is a sign of free thinking. In the Nation of Domeness, free thinking is not allowed. You are probably wondering how the Government ever gain full control over the people, I am here to tell you my story.

It all first started with the President, he started out as a side project in the early 1980's. Mr. President was born into a normal freethinking world. That is until the Government officials chose him, since his I.Q. was higher than most kids his age that were tested. He was the perfect candidate or test subject some people would say. As soon as he was able to go to school, he was taken away from his parents and sent to the best schools that money could buy. By the time that he was in high school, he had found a cure for every cancer that was out there. His college years were spent trying to find ways to get the United States to make peace with Iraq. After his graduation from college, he was already hired into office and by that time no one was ever going to argue with a child prodigy. Along with the fact that he made it to the point that the United States came first before any other nation's problems, he was loved and feared like God. No one argues with God.

Now we are controlled just like puppets because in my eyes, we were beyond ignorant to even question the authority of the Government. When they started the deamericanization of the country, first it was population control, and then they made it mandatory that you get a special license to have children. Child Protective Services had to deem you fit to be a parent, through the process of evaluation along with your genetic background and family history. If you were related to Ted Bundy or Albert Fish, there was without a doubt that you would not be granted a license. Therefore, in a way we were like China. Of course babies were born, but without this license the child was an illegal citizen, and to Uncle Sam the child was never born. Then there was the Food Control Act, it was a bill that passed the Senate and signed by the President. This allowed the Government to choose what food we ate. Fatty foods and all unhealthy foods were taken out of the people's diet. Fast food places tried to keep up with the law, but one by one, they all had to shut down to the point that there are no longer McDonalds or Taco Bell.

When the construction of the Dome began, no one argued. We were told that it was for our own protection and the safety of our health. Just like puppets, we were led by the strings that the Government held tightly in their hands. We all emptied our homes one day, left everything behind besides one bag of cloths that we were allowed to bring. One bag per person and that was it. People left their pets behind to fend for themselves. I can say on that day, I have never seen so many dogs and cats left out on the streets. I still remember as if it were yesterday, even though I was only a child. I still have a sour spot for my parents, because they would tell me stories of my grandparents. They called them the forever hippies, I always thought that hippies fought for peace and equality, and that they would teach their kids the same to fight back for what they thought was right and just. Not follow the unjust like robots.

Now we are just stuck in this man made bubble where the sun barely shines. It peaks beyond the glass roof that hangs over our heads. Sweet summer breezes are no longer felt, since the air is controlled. The new White House is nothing but a control system over this Dome. I often hear rumors that there are walls upon walls of security cameras that watch over their precious eco system, that was built. I know that there are little offices that are in the zone areas that control certain cameras at certain times. It's scary knowing that there is always someone watching your every move.

I'm number 578648548, my real name is Zack. Zack Helenkopf, I am fifteen years old am I am part of the last generation that was born as a free thinking American. There are not many of us left, since the people are controlled by fear and empty promises. In my head I am still the free thinker that I once was. The free thinker that my parents wanted me to be at one point, even though I am chipped and I have a barcode tattooed on the bottom of my wrist. The Government cannot control the way that I think inside my head, I still have that freedom. My parents are a part of the 90's generation, I often hear stories on how my parents could go anywhere that they pleased. They often tell me that they miss the way that grass felt on their bare feet. I can't even remember grass, I see pictures of it in the books that we are allowed to read at school, but I don't even know how it feels or even smells.

The Dome is nothing but concrete, besides a few flower decorations and trees, they were put there for false hope, so people can say, "Hey we have trees, it can't be that bad." But then again, that is another lie that people tell themselves on a daily basis. Somewhere in the Dome, there is a good amount of farmland. That I hear has grass. But because of the Food Control Act you had to be appointed to be a farmer. Since the food feeds the entire Dome because we are not allowed to eat in our house,everyone eats in a giant cafeteria depending on which zone you live in. Certain zones have certain cafeterias but everyone in the Dome eats at the same exact time every single day.

I often get tired of doing the same thing every single day. I know that I have no choice but to follow the rules but it still bugs me to the point, where I feel like ripping my own hair out sometimes. School is okay even though I sit there banging a pen against my head until I am allowed to leave. Even the school uniform drives me insane, considering every school in the dome has the same uniform. The only difference is that they have on it is the school's name. I often think I would get in trouble if I changed the uniform just a little bit but then again, I do not want to get in trouble. I do not want to disappear and I know my parents could not careless of the fact that their child was a trouble maker, or even an open free thinker.

Open free thinking is practically against the law, since we are controlled there are not any major crimes. Weed does not exist, people have tried to sneak it in the Dome but they couldn't get past the bag search at their arrival in the Dome. Drugs all together don't exist, since before the dome. People were overdosing on prescription medications, more than they were any other man made drug in the world. The Government appointed doctors to search for alternative medications that would help the people, without addicting traits or side effects. Murder was a thing of the past, how could you even get away with it? When someone is watching you all of the time.

Property being stolen was also a thing of the past, since people did not have anything to take anymore. Envy and greed were things of the past, all we really have left is the ability to free think. The Government made it a point that free thinking is against the law, the highest crime in this nation in fact. Since free thinking is against the law, people either did it in silence or they did not do it at all.

People in the Dome are robots, mindless little robots. If you really think about it, it's actually sad being told what to do and how to do it. Is that what God created humanity for? I wondered if we are just some sort of television show just for God to watch. He is either sitting there in disgust, shame, and humiliation. Or he is sitting there laughing and waiting for what is next, while biting his nails with his eyes glued to the television.

You could say that it was like a television show, due to the glass that was above our heads. Mom told me that the dome reminded her of a movie that she had once seen. It was about a person that lived in a dome, while the outside world watched his entire life, and he did not even know it. The movie starred Jim Carrey, but right now I cannot even think of the name of the movie. Since that I have not even seen it, it wasn't one of the movies that were on the Government approved list. She told me that the main character realized that his entire world was a lie and he wanted or got out of it. I believe that I haven't seen the movie because the Government doesn't want any of the people to get out of the dome.

I know that *V for Vendetta* is on the ban list considering the movie is mainly about freeing people from an unjust Government system. Our first year in the Dome, people wore the mask that is in the movie and protested, saying that the Dome is a huge jail system. Every single one of those people were sent to jail, because they were an endangerment to mankind and the future of the nation. No one has protested since then, no one really has fought back since 2028. I was only eight years old, but I still can remember the fights that broke out and all of the cops that took the people away.

In a way, America has fallen into its own holocaust, the people that rise up and rebel against what they thought was wrong. They disappear, no one knows where they go, or if they are ever coming back. We don't even know if they are alive or if they are dead, people are too afraid to even find out. I lost my Uncle and Aunt to the police about five years ago. My Aunt is my mother's baby sister, her and my Uncle wanted to have a child. They endured the entire process, only to find out that Child Protective Services did not see my Uncle fit to be a father. My Uncle, the most loving man in the world from what I can remember. Not being able to be a father? When my Aunt and Uncle found out that they were not allowed to have a legal child, they were furious and I really do not blame them. That's when my Aunt decided to go against Child Protective Services, her and my Uncle protested in front of the local office. The cops were called, I haven't seen them since. That is what happens when you speak out, that is what happens when you start to free think. You lose everything and everyone you ever loved.

I would wonder sometimes, what it was like before the Dome. When people were able to do what they wanted. A time when a hard working American was common, and the ability to think along with the ability to say whatever you wanted. A time when the American Flag was a symbol of courage, bravery, and a symbol that many men and women had fought for. Not just a symbol that was there just to be there, freedom was a thing that was taken for granted. Since people got used to having it, they really didn't realize what they had until it was gone. Like most things, you really don't know what you have until it's gone.

If you are wondering about religion in the Dome, the Government found a way to wipe that completely out. They in fact found a way or loophole I should say, that the Government could interfere with religion. They said that since we are all living under one nation, that we all should be treated equal. No one had special rights anymore, no special holidays, nothing. It didn't matter if you are white, black, or even green. You are going to be treated as equally as the person before, next, or behind you. People did not have any special names either, according to the Government. You are an equal American citizen and you will be treated as such. But the reality was, you are a controlled citizen of a Dome and everyone was treated equally. You have no rights, you cannot govern over your own life, your children's lives, or even your grandchildren's lives. That is if you are lucky enough to even have them in the first place.

CHAPTER TWO

The week started out just like any other week. Monday, since the dawn of time, or the dawn of Monday's, it is the most hated day of the week, month, and even year. My alarm clock went off at five thirty, like always. No matter how often I hit the snooze button, I could not escape the annoying beep telling me to wake up. I did not want to get out of bed and it took Mom screaming at me, for me to finally get out of bed. It took me a minute to finally get on my feet, and stagger across my bedroom to my dresser to get my school uniform. I rested my forehead, on the top of the dresser for a bit, asking myself why? Why do I have to get up so early? Why do I have to go to school? I mean school was not doing me any good anyways.

I got the uniform on and made my way to the bathroom to finish getting ready. While looking at myself in the mirror, I was tempted to make robot noises at myself. I know that I would get questioned, if I did. Since there is a camera behind the mirror, I would be looked at either as if I was stupid, or I would find myself in handcuffs being let out the front door. While my neighbors watched, considering that no one really had a house. People lived in apartment type buildings. It was really hard to keep secrets from everyone. People would know who you are, and your business even if you didn't know who they are at all.

After getting ready in the bathroom, I made my way into the livingroom. Mom was finishing getting ready herself. When she was done, I grabbed my jacket and school side bag. We made our way out of the building to go to the Cafeteria. Dad could not join us, since he was already out of the house and to his assigned job. Even though we all lived in a Dome, living was never free. People had assigned jobs, men always worked in some kind of factory, unless you worked for the Government in some way. Women worked in shops or as office clerks, that is until they got married, then they were forced to quit their job and to become a homemaker. Then later a possibly stay at home mom.

When Mom and I got into the cafeteria, there was already a long line of school kids with their mothers waiting to get breakfast. Even though the line was long, it went by really fast. At the cafeteria the plates were already made, so all the workers did was hand you a plate with food on it. What took longer was, when they had to scan your barcode on your wrist. After they scanned your wrist, the information went into the computer for data purposes, basically saying that you have gotten your food and also for their records, so they would know how much food they needed to make for the next morning. The Government valued the system, and they took it very seriously.

Today's breakfast was eggs, bacon with all of the fat cut off of it, hash browns, toast, and a glass of orange juice along with a glass of whole milk. This was not my favorite breakfast, I dreaded it when they served eggs, because they had no flavor and the little packets of salt and pepper that they gave you was not enough to add to the littlest bit of flavor, to such a horrible meal. The bacon was like biting into a piece of fried cardboard. Sometimes it was so rough, that it would cut the roof of your mouth, while you attempted to chew it. Please do not get me started on the hash browns, they were either too soggy to even eat them, or they were black and you didn't even want to touch them. By that time you already wasted all the salt that you had on the eggs. The only things that they didn't mess up or had any flavor was the milk and orange juice. You tried to make those last during the entire meal, but that usually never worked. You would choose hospital food over dome cafeteria food any day. I know that I would, if I had the choice but I don't even have that glorious choice.

After waiting in line and getting my wrist scanned, Mom and I found an empty table at the very edge of the Cafeteria. We put our trays down, and very slowly got into our seats. I could tell that mom was tired, she barely got enough sleep at night. Mom has sleeping problems, she refused to take the sleeping medications at night that the doctor gave her. I really do not blame her for not wanting to take them, although a person needs to sleep at night. Dad said that she would stay awake at night, until her body would shut down due to the lack of sleep but then it was too late and Mom would get an hour or two of sleep it she was lucky.

Sitting at the table, I was staring at my breakfast. Stirring it around with my fork, debating if I should take a bite of this so called meal. Mom, sitting there holding her cup of coffee in her hands, trying to grasp what energy that she had left.

"You should eat."

"I know Mom, but I'm not really all that hungry."

"If you don't eat, then they will think that something is wrong with you."

"Something will be wrong with me if I do eat this."

She sat back, covered her mouth and giggled a little bit. First laugh of the day, I've always got Mom to laugh in the morning. Her laugh always got my day going. To me it was my cup of coffee.

Even though Mom was right about eating, alot of the people were sent to the hospitals for not eating. They were automatically labeled with an eating disorder, and they were force fed. The doctors would shove a tube down their throat, which led down to the stomach. I only knew about it because some of my friend's parents had to go thru the process. Stories like that made you think twice about your actions. I felt like I had the tube down my throat when I ate breakfast. I often found myself, putting my hand to my mouth trying to keep the food down. It would come up and I would have to swallow it again. My stomach would toss and turn, at least a few times a week.

After breakfast, Mom and I went our separate ways, our "Goodbye" was at the table and our "See you later" was at the doors. I made my way to school when she walked back home. You walked everywhere you went, some people owned bikes if they were lucky enough to own one. Police and other Government Officials had electric cars. Me, I did not mind the walk I actually found it peaceful and it allowed me to think more than I could anywhere else. It seemed that I wasn't the only one that enjoyed the walk to school. My friend Adrian would meet me half way and we would walk to school with both of our heads down. I didn't know what he was thinking about, but there was nothing but bitter sweet silence the entire way. At least until the last minute, "So what do you think?" he asked. "Think what?" I answered, Adrian looked confused there for just a second.

"About what we are going to learn today?"

"Oh, well I don't know!"

Adrian would ask me that question every day, before school. I would give him the same answer, the real question he was trying to ask was. "What are you thinking?" I really wanted to tell him, what I was thinking every day. But I could not, things like that were hard to answer. Questions for me were never hard to answer, besides that one. Asking someone what they were thinking, is like asking a doctor to stop genetic birth defects before they even happen. Which is impossible, considering no one can stop nature even at its best times.

When we got to school, our friend Dan met us at the front door. Dan was a grade lower than us, but to me and Adrian it didn't matter, He still grew up with us Dan was also in the same building that I was. My parent's and Dan's mom often hung around each other. In addition the fact that both of our fathers worked at the same factory at one point. "Did you hear about Sarah?" asked Dan. "No, what about her?" Adrian said. "Well, you know that she was dating Jake for a few years right?" Dan said. I shook my head agreeing with Dan, since Sarah and Jake have been together for a few years. You would think that nothing would happen to them. Their names were the last names that you would ever expect to hear. "Sarah is pregnant!!" Rebecca screamed.

Rebecca is one of Sarah's best friends, plus she really likes Adrian and everyone knew it but him. She heard our conversation and blurted out the news, before Dan could break the silence. You could tell that Dan wanted to break the news, he wasn't pleased that Rebecca gossiped about it before he had the chance. Just the look on his face, told his story of disappointment alone. "Wait, Sarah is pregnant! How did that happen?" I said in shock. Rebecca started her sentence, then Dan quickly covered her mouth with the palm of his hand. "She stopped taking her birth control!" he shouted.

At a certain age, the Government made it mandatory for girls to take birth control. It usually started when they first started their period, or at the first sign of puberty. This originally started with the Obamacare plan. The Government paid for birth control, even though Obama didn't make it mandatory for girls to take birth control. That started when Obama's second term was over, and the President after him eliminated Obamacare. Although he kept some of the values, that Obama had made with the healthcare plan. They wanted to help eliminate teen pregnancies all together, you could say that it was the first key in the door to the first step of population control. Teen pregnancies cut down to about 98%. It took a few years, but 98% is better than 2%. Sarah is now a part of that 2%.

"What is going to happen to her?" Adrian asked. I just shook my head and shrugged my shoulders. We all knew what was going to happen to her. Even though she didn't report her pregnancy to her doctor, there was no chance that she could hide it for long. Eventually she would have to report it to her doctor. Then she would be reported to Child Protective Services and they would have to take action. Sarah would be sent to the nearest building that supports teen mothers. She would continue her education there, while getting everything that she needed for her and the baby. Once the baby is born, it gets chipped and put up for adoption. The baby would get adopted by parents who had the license, but could not have a child of their own. In rare instances, if the baby was not adopted. He or she would live in a home with other kids, that did not get adopted. They would live out their lives like the rest of us in that home.

I knew that most kids my age were sexually active. There was no point in escaping that, although you were not allowed to get married until after graduation, it did not stop teens from being adventurous.

Plus the fact that we learned in school about that over a hundred years ago, most girls got married at a young age. Along with having kids before they even hit their twenties. So the teens today, found ways to get away with it from their parents, and the Government no matter how much it was frowned upon. Plus there were certain spots that the Government couldn't watch at all times, if you snuck around enough. It was easy to get away with stuff like that. You also had to know the when, where, time, and how. That itself took very careful planning.

I started feeling bad for Sarah, because not only did she have no choice in any matter. But now she has no choice in something, that generations before us had the freedom to do. I, myself could not bear the fact, that I would have to give away a part of me. I wonder what Jake thought about all of this, did he even know he was going to be a father? Only time would tell.

After that gossip session, the first school bell rang. The first bell of the day, letting us know that we have five minutes to get to class. It was more like seven or eight, because instead of the teacher taking attendance, you have to scan your wrist at the door, it was the easiest way for the school to take attendance, instead of the teacher wasting time to mark who was in class and who was not in class. The lessons in class started faster too, my school day started with Mrs. Keen. She taught history, it was rather boring. Like most Government Officials, teachers had to be appointed. To be a female teacher was a rare thing too, also a great accomplishment.

"Okay, everyone please get your notebooks out along with your text books. Today we are going to start with the Great Depression" she said. Everyone in class got their books out and turned to the appropriate page that had the title "The Great Depression" as the chapter headliner. Mrs. Keen waited until everyone was on the same page, then she told us. "Read this chapter, after you are done answer the questions at the end. Then we will go over it when everyone is done." I thought to myself "Oh great! I hate silent reading." That is practically how Mrs. Keen started out every week, then we would discuss the topic that we had just read for the entire week. History is my favorite subject, reading on the other hand was my least favorite subject.

I sat at my desk, looking down at my book. Pretending to read, while pressing my pen against my temple. I sat there wondering what it was like during The Depression. What it would be like to openly speak out against the Government freely and without fear. I knew that my great grandparents grew up during that time. I would really like to ask them, what it was like. They died a long time ago and the only way that I could ask them is when I am on the other side, and free myself. That wouldn't be for a long time though.

Before I knew it, the second class bell began to ring. I didn't even read the chapter, or even answer the questions at the end of the chapter. I quickly looked at the end of it, and there was 40 questions. "40 questions!!" I thought to myself. I packed my books away, while I wallowed in my own stupidity. I am very happy that Mrs. Keen gives you until Friday, to turn in all of your homework along with the classwork. I think it is because you had to write down the question, and the answer in your notebook. That was a few hours of work alone.

My second class was math with Mr. Smith unlike Mrs. Keen, he wanted your classwork, as soon as you were done. It was not simple math either Mr. Smith loved to make your brain hurt. While you were trying to figure out the multiple problems on the board and if you got one wrong, you had three chances, to get it right. "Three chances and you are out!" he said. The out part meant you were going to stay with him after school, until it was dinner time. Mr. Smith's after school classes were heart breaking because he drilled you until he saw fit. He watched you like a hawk, he watched over you making sure you followed his steps to the problem. If you did it in a way that he did not like, or got some part of it wrong. He would grab the paper away from you, rip up the paper, and then crumble it up into a little ball. Then shoot it into the trashcan, as if it was a basketball and then tell you to do it all over again.

The longer it took you to solve the problem, the longer you stayed there. If you didn't get it done by dinner time, then you had no choice but to stay the next day after school. This is one of the reasons, plus many others why Mr. Smith was the least favorite teacher in the entire school. I dreaded his class, the only reason I enjoyed it was because of Sam. I have this puppy dog crush on her I could not even talk to her without stuttering like an over exhausted fool. The fact that I couldn't say, what I really wanted to say to her. Made me feel like a complete idiot. I needed a good smack in the head, to make me come back into reality whenever she came around. That is what Adrian was for, since he is in the same class. He acts like the little voice, in the back of my head or he would actually hit me in the back of the head and tell me not to be so stupid. Adrian was my voice of reason.

I sat down at my seat in the class, Adrian sat right next to me. We both got our notebooks out, looked at the board, and started working on the problems for the part of class. Unlike most teachers, Mr. Smith not only wanted your name on the top of the paper, but he also wanted your number right next to your name, so it looked like this "Zack Helenkopf-578648548." Mr. Smith said that since it was his math class, that all numbers are important. Also that it was important to learn our number, and to memorize it. He made sure that we knew our number by heart, and if we didn't write it down on our papers, we would get in a lot of trouble.

I sat there working on the problems, writing each step down. I felt like that it is more of a headache, than it should have been. I began clicking my pen, thinking of each step that I needed to take. In reality I was breaking the silence in the class, silence drove me nuts. I had to click my pen or I would go insane. I took a quick glance over at Adrian, he was biting the eraser on his pencil. "Are you okay?" I asked, he didn't even budge when I asked him. So I bumped him on his shoulder. I finally got Adrian's attention, "What?" he whispered. "Are you okay? You look a bit troubled there" I whispered back. Adrian shook his head no, then got back to his paper. I got back to my work as well I found myself biting my lip while I was writing. I looked like a writer stuck in a writer's block group, or the fact that I was majorly focused. This was just my body's way of showing it.

When I got done with my paper, I took a deep breath, covered my face with my hands, and thanked myself for getting it done. When I took my paper to Mr. Smith's desk, he looked up at me, "Are you done?" he asked, I shook my head in a yes motion and Mr. Smith took a glance over my work. "Well done Zack" he said, that was my cue to go sit back down at my seat. It also meant that I did it right the first time, and I didn't have to do the problems over again. I did not have to stay after school either, this time. The nightmare of this class was finally over, I was screaming in joy, deep inside my head.

On my way back to my seat, I felt like dancing. Actually I felt like a little kid, who just got a puppy. That is how I felt every time Mr. Smith gave his motion of approval. I can tell you that I spent too many times after school. Dealing with the constant headache, along with his harshness and cruelty that he called teaching. I pity the poor soul that had to deal with Mr. Smith on a daily basis. I survived another class of his for another day, which was something to be happy about. Now it was time for me to lay my head down, on the table at my seat and wait, for the bell to ring.

For what seemed like an eternity of waiting, the bell finally rang. I quickly got up, put my bag to my side, and rushed my happy self out the door. On the way to my next class, I ran into Dan. He asked me about Mr. Smith's math problems for today, I told him that it was major headache. It really didn't matter to him, because Dan is extremely smart when it came to math even smarter than me. He was amongst the very few that never had to stay after school. I often teased him by calling him one of the gifted ones, and that I was not worth of his friendship. Dan would get mad at me every time, as I would laugh. Even though Dan is a grade younger than me, his talent in mathematics did not go unnoticed. I really wouldn't be surprised, if he reached college level math by the time that he graduates.

After talking to Dan for a couple of minutes, I made my way to my next class. It was physical education and it was one of the classes that I looked forward to more than Mr. Smith's class. Not because of the girls that were in the class, but it was a class that we were allowed to have fun in. Along with the fact that if we got hurt, it did not get reported. So if you threw a ball and it hit someone in the face, you didn't get in trouble. It was considered an accident. Today, I knew that we would be playing basketball, I am actually good at it too. I take pride in my jump shot.

The only thing that I did not like about the class, was the fact that a kid named Mark is in this class. Mark is the kid that nobody likes because he has a nasty attitude towards everyone, including the teachers in the school. Everyone, plus myself questioned how he hasn't been dragged out by the police yet. Mark is that type of kid, the kid who bullied anyone for anything. Today, Mark decided that I was going to be his next victim. He had tripped me, when we got on the gym floor. "Walk much!" he laughed. That is when I decided that Mark should get a taste of his own medicine. My dad always told me that I should not be the one to throw the first punch, but to always finish the job even though fights are extremely rare in the

Dome. Fighting would still happen, it was always the person who protected themselves, that never got in trouble.

I didn't throw the first punch, but I would finish the job. I just have to wait, for the perfect opportunity to do so. The joyous moment came when Mr. Clyde, the gym teacher put me and Mark on different teams. The last straw is when Mark threw a basketball against my back when I was going to the opposite side of the gym than him. "I called heads up, I thought you heard me!" Mark smirked. All I could think in my head was, "Game on!" That is what it was nothing but a big game. A game of basketball began, and it seemed like it was me and Mark in the court all by ourselves. I waited until he ran past by me, I ran up right next to him. Mark is now sandwiched between me and the wall. There was one of my teammates in front of him and another one behind him. I checked him into the wall as hard as I could. His head, bounced off of the wall and he fell on the floor. When he fell, everyone stopped to watch what was going on. Mark was as limp as a noodle, on that gym floor. "What happened!" yelled Mr. Clyde. We all just shrugged our shoulders, everyone knew what I did. They didn't want to tell on me, I had bullied the bully. Mr. Clyde lifted Mark into a sitting position. There was a little pool of blood where Mark's head was.

Mr. Clyde looked up and pointed to one of my classmates. "Go to the office, tell them to call the hospital. We have someone extremely hurt over here." He demanded, "Class is over." The class ended faster than it had begun, I'm just happy that no cameras were able to record what happened. I made sure that the spot I slammed Mark against the wall was a spot that was not visible by them. I know for a fact, that I could have gotten in a lot of trouble because of what I had done. Part of me cared, the other half didn't care, at all. By the time the ambulance came, Mark was already awake. He was really confused about what had happened. He was also confused as to why he was strapped down to a stretcher and being taken to the hospital. I don't think that he even knows that he is bleeding out of his head, and the fact that there could possibly more damage to his brain than there already is.

Mr. Clyde's class was just before lunch. Since class ended earlier than normal, the entire class was able to go to lunch early. We made our way to the school cafeteria, the food was exactly like the Dome's Cafeteria food. Nasty with just a pinch of vile, and you had to force yourself to get past the smell. A lot of the time, you'd rather bite your tongue until it bled. So you didn't have to eat it, I sat there quietly, until my lunch hour came. Adrian, Dan, Sam, and Rebecca have the same lunch hour as I do. We all sat at the same table, every day. After I got my tray of food, I sat down at the table. I began stirring the food around my plate with a plastic fork. I waited until everyone got to the table, I looked up, and gave my usual greeting smile. "So did you really, bash Mark's head against the wall in gym class?" Sam asked. I looked up at her, "How did you know?" I am a little confused on how Sam knew about it when she wasn't even in my class. "The entire school knows!" Adrian shouted in a whisper. I slapped the palm of my hand, against my forehead. It was only a matter of time, before the teachers would find out about what I had done. I would get reported to the Principal, then he would have to report me to the police. Who knows what would happen to me at that point. The last thing that I wanted, was to get into trouble. I tried very hard to stay out of it. Being turned in, was the last thing that I wanted at this time. All I wanted to do was to teach someone else a lesson and that was it. I am no longer the hero at that point and I wasn't the bully that bullied the bullies, I am the bully. Being a bully was not the reputation that I wanted either.

A thousand things were going on in my head. " I wanted to teach him something!" I blurted. Everyone's eyes got big, what did I just do! I had admitted to the fact that I purposely sent someone to the hospital. All because I wanted to teach them a lesson. I might as well have turned myself in, along with put the handcuffs on myself. I could walk in the jail cell, and close the door behind me. That is what I was pretty much, doing to myself. All I could thing is "Oh God please help me know!" at that point, I couldn't eat at all. I got my tray, got up from my seat, and threw my food away. I made my way out of the cafeteria, to the nearest bench that I could sit down alone at. The only thing that I could think about was what have I done? The thought repeated in my head, over and over again. I had a broken record, repeating itself inside my head. It was also a mixture of guilt, worry, and shame that turned itself into a big bomb. That exploded, inside my head. Adrian sat down right next to me, "Zack are you okay?" he asked. "Man I feel like I'm going to be sick" I replied. My stomach was turning a million times over and over again. I was letting my emotions, get the best of me.

Adrian looked at me, "Mark got what he deserved! It's about time someone stood up to him." Adrian said.

"That's not what I'm worried about"

"Then what is it?"

"Adrian you know exactly what happens to people around here, when they get in any sort of trouble"

"Yes, I do. But you have nothing to worry about"

"Now how do you know that? I'm only fifteen, I don't need this kind of attention right now"

"Zack, what do you think is going to happen? You think that they will take you away for you to rot? Where ever they send people?"

"Well yea, I mean that will happen. If I do get reported"

"There is the word that I was waiting for, Zack"

"What word?"

"The big "if""

All I did was sit there and shake my head. Adrian was right. The word "If" was a big one. It didn't stop me from feeling sick though. After lunch, I went into the school office. "Can I go home? I feel really sick" I told the secretary. "What's wrong?" she asked, "The food is not agreeing with me right now." I lied, she looked at me for a minute. "Sign yourself out, and scan your code so we know that you left" she snarled. I think that she knew that I was lying to her. The school didn't take any chances, when it came to kids being sick. The students signed themselves out when they hit high school. It is one of the perks to being older. You could lie about being sick, and you could automatically go home. You don't want to abuse it though, if you played sick enough, instead of going home. You ended up going to the hospital. You would end up getting tested by doctors. I rarely was sick as it is, so I got to go home.

I quietly made my way out of the school's front doors. I feel like I am walking the path of shame, even though I wasn't the only one walking around. It felt like I was, I am all alone in my head. Mothers with their little kids are out right now, either walking around to get out of the home or they were just that bored. Cops were also walking around, monitoring the area, keeping people in line. My heart raced every time I passed one, I am just waiting for one of them to stop and ask me why I wasn't at school. But every time I passed one, they didn't even bother. They would look at me, and nod their head. I really look as sick as I felt? Maybe it is the reason, why a cop did not even bother to ask me. Or maybe for once they had better things to do, than bother their time with me. I would never know, I am glad that I wasn't stopped on my way home.

I finally made it to my building. I walked to the elevator, got in, and pressed the eighth floor button. When I got to my floor, I walked to the front door, scanned my wrist, and waited to hear the sound of the door unlocking. As I walked in, Mom was sitting there on the couch, watching the Government recommended television. She looked up at me when she heard the door close behind me. "What are you doing home, so soon?" she asked. "I really don't feel good Mom" I replied. She didn't ask me what was wrong, the conversation was over. I put my bag near the door, and made my way to my bedroom. Taking a deep breath, I took off my jacket. I didn't even bother putting it on my dresser. I threw it on the floor, I didn't even care at that point. I am the cleanest person in the world. If there was something out of order in my room, it drove me nuts to the point that I had to fix it. For me to just lay something like that on the floor, without it bothering me, there is something really wrong.

I sat down at the edge of my bed, placed my hand at the top of my head, and moved it to the bottom of my neck. I fell back on my bed, laying there staring at the ceiling. Closing my eyes, I wished that I were somewhere else. I wish that I was out of the Dome, out of this Country, and off this Planet! I knew that it was never going to happen, I am a good dreamer though. I fell asleep, only to be woken up by Dad. Telling me that Mom and him were going to the Cafeteria for dinner. He asked me if I wanted to come with them. I shook my head no and laid back into the pillow. How could I even eat with the way that I was feeling? No matter how much my stomach begged for food, I'd rather starve. I ended up forcing myself back to sleep for the rest of the night.

CHAPTER THREE

I woke up that morning, with the same amount of guilt that I had gone to bed with the night before. There is no way that I could get it out of my head, not even for one second. I woke up before my alarm went off, so I had the pleasure of lying in my bed. Only to wait until that annoying beep echoed in my room. My stomach stopped turning, it was replaced with the feeling of emptiness, along with the sounds of hunger growls. Right now I am starving. I feel like I can eat an entire cow at this point, if the chance was ever given to me. I would do it without question.

The alarm started going off. "Here we go." I whispered to myself and I threw the covers off of me to the edge of the bed. I got up, and put my feet on the cold floor. I did not want to get out of my bed considering that I could either keep or lose my sanity. Without anyone knowing, or even bothering me. Even though there is a camera in my room, I could turn away from it, and stay awake when the person was watching thought that I was still sleeping. I staggered my way to my dresser, got my school uniform, and got ready for the day. While brushing my teeth, I looked at myself in the mirror, I realized that I am a different person than I was yesterday. I have changed, I couldn't decide if it was either in a good or bad way. I am not the same Zack that I used to be.

Mom and I went to the cafeteria like always. Today's breakfast is pancakes with maple syrup, toast, sausage, apple juice, and milk. The smell of it teased my stomach, like a little kid teased a dog with a bone. I could not wait to eat it, despite how nasty it tasted. I was going to eat it all, that's exactly what I did too. When we got to the table, Mom couldn't even reach her seat, before I started shoveling food into my mouth. For a minute she just looked at me. "I see that you're feeling better." I smiled at her with a mouth full "mmmhmm!" She giggled at me a little bit, I think that she is happy to the fact that I was inhaling food after skipping dinner last night.

After breakfast, I made my usual walk to school. I met Adrian and Dan at the doors as usual. "What happened to you yesterday?" Dan asked. I told him that I felt sick, and that I went home for the rest of the day. I didn't think that he believed me, I don't blame him either. I wouldn't even believe myself after what happened yesterday. I am just wishing that the gossip didn't reach the teacher's ears. If it did, then today is going to be a really rough day for me. I have a lot of stress on me as it is right now, I did not want to add anymore.

Mrs. Keen's class was like normal, even though it got interrupted right in the middle of it. There was a new student that came into the class that day. She wasn't like any normal student either. In fact, she was new to the Dome too. Her name is Elizabeth, she had moved to the Dome from England. Foreigners are extremely rare, other Countries still remained free. Their people did not want to come over here. They had to be really stupid for wanting to live in this place. Mrs. Keen placed Elizabeth behind me, I had refrain myself from wanting to ask her so many questions. Instead I turned around and introduced myself. If someone was going to be friends with her, it was me. I welcomed her into my group of friends, which it was really easy to do.

The first half of the morning was a breeze. Lunch time on the other hand was kind of difficult, because of the silence, since no one said a word at the table. That was until I saw Elizabeth, looking around the cafeteria for a place to sit. She looked confused, it must have been hard for her. She did not know anyone in here. You could tell that she is a very shy girl. I got up from my seat, and walked up to her. "It's scary huh?" I asked. She looked at me, "It is actually truly terrifying." I told her that she could sit at the same table that I was at. She looked at me, while we were both making our way to the table. When we sat down, everyone introduced themselves. "Hello, my name is Elizabeth." She said shyly. "You're not from here are you?" asked Adrian. "No...Adrian, her English accent doesn't give it away!" snarled Dan. Elizabeth laughed, "No, my Grandpa lives here. My parents moved to England when I was a baby." "So why did you move here?" Rebecca asked. "Well, my parents died in a car crash months ago and since my Grandpa is my only relative I have left, I really had no choice but to move here." Elizabeth paused, "It took a couple of months for the Government to grant my Grandpa custody of me, also with allowing me to come here in the first place. Trust me this is the last place that I ever wanted to come to."

We all looked at her. I don't even want to know the pain that she was feeling when she lost her parents and the fact that she had no choice but move to this place, that she didn't want to be at. And to lose the freedom that you had your entire life must have been hard too. The rest of lunch was spent in silence. Elizabeth just sat there playing with her food, I don't think that she was used to this type of food yet. It would take time before she got hungry enough to eat it.

When lunch was over, I went into my English class. The teacher is Mr. Johns, his class was okay. The class spent most of the time writing in our notebooks about a subject that he picked out. The rest of the time was spent working on grammar. When he had seen that I was in the class, he called me up to the desk, "Why were you not in class yesterday?" he asked. I explained to him that I didn't feel good, and that I went home. I also apologized that I had missed his class, and that I will make up for yesterday's assignment. Mr. Johns agreed with me, then he gave me the subject topic that he had the class do yesterday. He also told me that it had to be at least three or four pages long. I had my work cut out for me, because today's subject had to be six pages long. Altogether, I had to write ten pages within a half hour. Also, have it turned in by then. Yesterday's subject was easy, I had to explain what I did over the weekend. I like subjects like that because it was mainly free writing. Also I did the same thing every weekend. That was spend my days with Adrian and Dan playing court hockey or basketball, maybe even sometimes football.

The next subject, the subject for today was "What does freedom mean to you?" I really didn't know how to answer it. Or even write about it without getting in trouble. It is a trick question, what I really wanted to write I couldn't. I really wanted to say, that we have no freedom. If I even wrote that, I would get into some serious trouble. No matter if it was the truth or not, plus the fact that I didn't even know what true freedom was. I wrote down some over dramatic lie on the paper, saying that we have freedom now. My head actually hurt from creating the lie. It was either lie to get the work done, or tell the truth and get in trouble for it.

I am rather happy that the time came for the class to end. A sigh of relieve came as soon as the bell rang. It was time for my next class, which was science. In that class, we learned about organisms along with how things are created, and the theory of evolution. Mr. Hibs made the class interesting, since he made it very clear that the human evolution dawned from apes. Also, that their genetic background is very similar to ours. He often said that science is boring and that he hated it as a kid. He wanted to make things fun and that is exactly what he did.

The end of the school day came, the bell rang letting us know that it was either time to go home or to go where ever. I ended up waiting for Dan and Adrian outside the school. I wanted to see if they wanted to hang out after school, like we always do. The question was, what did we want to do after school? After a little debate, we decided that we wanted to play basketball in the court behind the school. It was easy to get teams together too. There were a lot of teens that did not want to go home after school. They would either hang out on the bleachers at the court, or play some kind of sport on the court grounds. While we were walking to the back of the school. Elizabeth ran up beside me, "Hello!' she giggled. "Hi" I giggled back.

"Sooo… What is it that you guys do around here?"

"Well this is it"

"Really? There has to be something more exciting than this"

"Nope, this is it"

The look of disappointment shadowed Elizabeth's face. When we got to the court, she had found a spot for herself. While me, Dan, and Adrian gathered up players for our team. While playing a game of basketball, I couldn't help but think about Elizabeth sitting on the bleachers all by herself. She had to be lonely. No one even bothered talking to her either, I glanced over at her. She was writing something down in her notebook. You could tell that she was really focused on what she was writing down.

After the game, I walked over and sat down right next to her. She stopped writing, then she looked up at me. She smiled, greeting me in a friendly manner. "What are you working on?" I asked her. Instead of telling me, she handed me her notebook. Elizabeth was working on the same English question that I had worked on earlier. She explained that freedom is being able to do whatever you wanted to do. To say what you want to say. What you wanted to do, you would have the ability to do so when you desired. She also explained that this meaning of freedom was no longer taught and that we are tagged like animals. That we are also caged like animals with no hope or desire to ever get out of the cage.

After reading what she had written down, I wanted to tell her that she was right about everything. But instead I told her that she could not write about it and that if she turned the paper in. She would get in a lot of trouble I ripped the paper out of her notebook, folded it up, and stuck it in my pocket. "Why do you guys willingly live like this?" she asked. I had to sit there and really think about it, "Because people are too scared about what would happen to them if they questioned it" I murmured.

"Is this the life that you have grown a custom too? To live like animals?"

"Well no, I mean it does look like it. But we don't have helmets on our heads that tell the Government what we are thinking."

"No you don't, in England we are allowed to do what we wanted when we want."

"Please tell me more about England" I said, Elizabeth looked at me like I asked her a million questions. She began to tell me about the house that she lived in. She explained it in such detail, to the point that I was able to picture it in my head when I closed my eyes. It was a brick house, very old looking. The door was in the middle with a window on each side. Three windows on top for the second story. A chimney at each end of the house, the roof was as black as the night's sky. The house was on a huge piece of farm land. She told me that there was a barn about a half of a mile away from the house. Her dad raised cows, chickens, horses, and pigs. I could only imagine that there was never a dull moment on the farm. Elizabeth also told me that she missed the way that her mother's cooking would fill the house with all kinds of different smells. She always knew when her mom was baking pies. When the scents of apples and cinnamon would fill the house, she would rush down to the kitchen every time. She would always have to wait for the apple pie to cool down enough to eat. Most of all, she missed her parents. Tears swelled up in her eyes when she started talking about them.

A tear started going down her face, it dripped onto the skirt of her school uniform. I put my arm around her, trying to give her comfort. Elizabeth wiped the tears from her eyes, than began to scratch at her wrist. "You know they are going to have to redo that barcode again if you scratch it off" I whispered. She giggled, looked up at me, and mouthed "Thank you." We sat there for a little bit in silence, she was staring out into the court. Her face had an empty expression on it. "So… What zone do you live in?" I blurted out to break the silence. "Zone 52" she said. "Really? That is the same zone that I live in!" I don't know what had taken over me, I was excited that she lived in the same zone that I did. That also meant that we ate in the same Cafeteria.

Thinking about food, I looked down at my watch. It was dinner time, I got up and asked Elizabeth if she would accompany me on the walk to the Cafeteria. She agreed, so like a gentlemen, I extended my arm out to her, for her to wrap hers around mine. "Oh, what a gentlemen" she giggled. My face turned ten shades of red, "You know what Zack, I like you!" she shouted. I was blown back by what she had said. A girl likes me! The planets must be aligned or I am dreaming. We walked to the cafeteria and then we parted ways to meet up with our families. We agreed to meet each other, later on that night.

At dinner, Dad asked me about the girl that I was walking with. I told him about Elizabeth, and that she was from England. "Do you like her?" he asked. I didn't even know how to answer his question. I mean, I just met her today. How could I determine that if I liked her or not. Elizabeth is very smart, pretty, and we do get along very well. I thought for a minute, "Yes I do" I blurted, while trying to shove food in my mouth. So that if Dad asked me another question, I had an excuse that my mouth is beyond full and that I couldn't talk with food in my mouth. Dad just laughed at me, "Honey just leave him alone, Zack is still young" Mom said. That was also Dad's hint not to say another word. Mom was Dad's voice of reason. Like Adrian was mine.

After dinner, I walked home with my parents like usual. When we got home, I went into my room and got some comfortable clothes on. I walked out of my room into the living room, to find my parents watching television "Hey Mom, I am going out for a bit. I will be back later," I said. "Okay Zack, just make sure that you are home before curfew" Mom said. Mom didn't even bother asking me where I was going or who I was going with. I am glad that my parents trust me that much, plus it helped that nothing bad happened around here.

I left my house, made my way to the building doors, and waited for Elizabeth. I had told her earlier to meet me in my building and what building that I lived in. Since she lived a few buildings over, the walk for her wasn't really that far. I waited for a little while before she showed up. She apologized for not coming sooner. She had a hard time convincing her Grandpa to let her go out. "So what are we going to do?" she asked. "Well I don't know" I replied. I really didn't know what to do. Usually after dinner, I stayed home with my parents. I either stayed in my room and worked on homework, or I watched television with my parents. This is my first time ever going out after dinner, there was also a curfew for every single person in the Dome. No one could be out of their home past ten. If you were, then you got into a lot of trouble.

"Let's go to the park!" I told her. Elizabeth nodded her head and smiled. There is a park not too far from my building. It was the spot where mothers took their kids during the day. Myself and everyone else joked about it, saying that it was the spot that mothers could get their sanity back. At night, the park was completely empty, the perfect place for me and Elizabeth to hang out without screaming kids, or being bothered by people for a few hours. Again I found myself being the gentlemen, lending my arm out to Elizabeth. That wasn't before I opened the door for her, when we walked out of the building.

As we were walking, Elizabeth started humming a tune. "Is the silence bothering you?" I laughed. "Yes, it actually is!" she smirked, the silence drove me crazy too. I did not know what to talk about, I felt like I had a frog in my throat. I didn't want to make myself look foolish, and get all choked up in front of her. When we got to the park, Elizabeth let go of my arm and ran over to the swings. "I feel like a kid again!" she screamed. I found a seat on the slide across from her. I just looked at her, she was glowing. Elizabeth looked a lot happier than she did at the court earlier. "Zack sit next to me please!" she pouted. "Okay…" I blurted. I got up, walked over to the swing next to her, and I sat down. I started swinging, I was never really a fan of swings. Even when I was a kid, Mom also kept me inside because of the protesters outside. They would often get violent. It was very dangerous for anyone to go outside at that time. My childhood was spent indoors. Mom tried as hard as she could to make the inside fun. There was not much that you could do though.

Elizabeth and I stayed on the swings for a little while, there really was not that much talking between us. She was enjoying being a kid again way too much, to even notice that there wasn't a conversation at all. It didn't bother me either, I enjoyed her company. As I looked down at my watch, I had seen that it was past ten. I got up and told Elizabeth that we had to go. She was confused at first, then she realized that it was past curfew. She had asked me to walk her, to her building. Since she did not want to walk by herself. I couldn't blame her either, she didn't know the short cuts like I did. Along with the fact that I could get around hiding from the cops. Dan was notorious for sneaking out past curfew, or even staying out past it. He had taught me the short cuts and the ways to stay in the dark.

We walked through alleyways, at each corner I made her stay behind me. As I looked around for cops, made sure it was clear. We made our way through it. It seemed like we were mice in a maze. Sneaking our way to where ever we were going. We just had to make sure that there was no cats around. We moved as quiet as mice too.

When we got to her building, there where cops at the doors. They were just standing there. "Don't worry, there is a backdoor" I told her. One of the cops must have heard me, I could hear him coming towards us. We were at the side of her building in the alleyway. I quickly grabbed her hand, and ran behind the huge air vent. I could see the beams of the flash light hit the wall of the building next to us. We waited until he was gone, Elizabeth was behind me when I peaked over the corner to make sure that the cop was gone. Then I pointed at the back of the building, "let's go" I whispered. I got Elizabeth to the backdoor. I am glad that I had my wallet with me that night, because Dan gave me small tools to pick locks, I remembered that I had put them in my wallet.

After I got done picking the lock to the backdoor, I slowly opened it for Elizabeth. Before she went in, she put both of her hands on each side of my face and kissed me on the forehead. "Thank you" she said, when she went inside. I quietly closed the door behind her, I couldn't believe that she kissed me. It wasn't a kiss, kiss, but it was still a kiss. My heart started beating faster, my stomach had butterflies in it, and a big smile found its way on my face. Her kiss was unexpected, but I'm glad it happened. I leaned against the backdoor, slid down it until I hit the ground, and sat there in utter bliss. Is this what puppy love felt like? If so, I like it!

Eventually I got up and snuck my way back home. When I walked through the front door, Mom was waiting for me. She wasn't happy either, she started yelling at me. Saying that I was very lucky that I didn't get caught. In her voice you could tell that there was a mixture of her being angry with me, and being worried about me. All I could do was tell her that I was sorry and that it wouldn't happen again. She made me promise that it would never happen again. I knew that it was a promise that I couldn't keep even if I wanted to. Being with Elizabeth was too much fun for me to even give up. If it meant that I had to break the rules to do it, I would. I didn't even care if I got caught, because it would be worth it.

After screaming at me, Mom told me to go to bed. She also told me, that she loves me. She also apologized for yelling at me. I knew that she was just being my mom, her job was also to worry about the ones that she loves. No matter how much she denies it, I still knew the truth. I loved her for it too. I walked into my room and dove onto my bed. I didn't even bother getting myself ready, or even getting the covers ready I just laid there, thinking about the day. Elizabeth, almost getting caught, and how worried Mom was. I was mostly thinking about Elizabeth and her kiss. That sweet kiss that moment kept on replaying in my head until I fell asleep.

CHAPTER FOUR

The next morning there was a loud knock at the door. It had woken up everyone, possibly the neighbors too, it was that loud. I laid in bed hoping that it wasn't what I was thinking it could possibly be. It was, the cops were at the door asking for me. Mom led them into my room, four cops were hovering over me, telling me to get up. When I did they did not hesitate to put the handcuffs on me. They led me out to the living room, I watched Mom's eyes follow me while tears flowed from them. I couldn't even look at her I was paying for the night before. They led me out the front door, and out of my building. There was an audience in front of the building. I was extremely ashamed of myself. I didn't even want to be alive right now.

The officer that led me to the cop car, opened the door. He grabbed me by the shirt and the rim of my pants, lifted me up off of the ground and threw me in the back of the cop car. I hit my head on the door on the other side. I looked at him in hate as he shut the door at my feet. I laid there as the two officers got in the car. I didn't even say a word when they started the car up. They drove to the police station. It is a huge building that I never wanted to go in, even though I passed by the building on my walks to school. When we got into the garage underneath the building, a few officers were waiting by the main doors. An officer opened the car door, grabbed me by my feet and pulled me out of the car. He helped me to get on my feet and then grabbed my arm, only to push me inside the building. There was a desk right by the doors. The officer took the handcuff off of my right arm and he forced me to scan my barcode. After I was scanned in, he put the handcuff back on my wrist. He led me into a room, it was dark with only a little bit of light, just enough to see. He took the handcuffs off of me, shoved me in the room and closed the door behind me.

I stood there, hearing him lock the door. I wanted to bang my head against the wall, to knock myself out. The room did not have any furniture, so the only place that I could sit was on the floor. I laid down on that cold floor in the middle of the room, looking up at the ceiling. I started banging the back of my head against the floor. Thinking about what I got in trouble for. It was either one of the two things, sending Mark to the hospital or my night out with Elizabeth last night. If it was either one, I am in a good amount of trouble for it.

A few hours passed and it seemed like forever. The sound of someone unlocking the door buzzed in my ears so I quickly sat up to see who was coming through that door. An officer came in with a chair, he placed it right in front of me. Behind him was a woman, she wasn't a cop, but she was dressed up in a suit. The suit alone gave it away, she was someone important. The officer left after he placed the chair while the woman sat down. She had a file in her hand, along with a notebook and a pen. The woman was young, she had an innocent look to her. I did not know whether to hate her or pity her because she works for the Government. "So Zack

Helenkopf, do you know why you are here today?" she asked. Her voice is very soft, it had a kind tone to it. I shook my head no, waiting for her to tell me why I was even there in the first place. She gave out a little sigh, then she opened the folder that she had in her hand.

She pulled out a picture, it was a picture of me from last night. Someone was monitoring the cameras in my building when I got home.

"Zack, what were you doing out last night past curfew?"

"I couldn't sleep, so I went out for a walk."
"If you have a sleeping problem, Zack you should go see a doctor."

"It was just last night, I swear."

"Was there anybody with you?"

I told her no, I lied to a Government Official. I wanted to protect Elizabeth. If the women knew the truth, then she would have gotten Elizabeth locked up for sure. Then who knows what they would have done with her. The woman looked at me, "Are you sure Zack, you know that lying to me will get you into more trouble" she snarled. "Yes, I am sure. I was alone last night," I snapped back. The woman got up from her chair, "Alright Zack, since this really didn't do any damage, and since this is your first time getting into trouble, I will call your mother to get you out of here."

She also told me to sit tight because it would take more than a minute for the paper work to get through. "We are going to be watching you!" she barked with those words. I knew now that I am really under the watchful eye of the Government. It was a few more hours before mom got there. She was waiting by the front doors for me. The first thing that she did was hug me, the hug was so tight that she could have squeezed the air out of me. She was happy that she didn't lose me I was happy that I didn't lose her.

When I got out, it was lunch time and I was starving. I was not given any food while I was in that room, my stomach was eating itself. "The officer at the desk told me that they already called you off of school" Mom said. I was happy that she had said that, because I really did not feel like dealing with the people at school right now. "Can we go to the cafeteria please?" I asked her. Mom just looked at me and smiled. As we were walking, I apologized for what had happened this morning. Mom just looked at me and said, "You're out that's all that matters right now." She was right, nothing else mattered at this time. Besides getting food into my stomach.

After lunch, Mom and I watched some television Mom liked to watch educational shows, mainly history which they would talk about the 90's and the early 2000's. Even though they only showed things about the Government during these times, she still liked watching it. I watched television with her until the time that school was let out. I asked her if I could go meet Dan at the court behind the school. She agreed, even though she hesitated a little bit. Then she told me that I had no choice but to stay home after dinner tonight. I didn't argue with her, I couldn't especially with what happened this morning. Plus the fact that I am now being watched more than ever. Made me want to follow the rules down to a "T."

I am going to be a good boy, if that kept Mom happy. I got my jacket on and walked out the door. I was walking to the school, I saw the same officers that took me to the police station this morning. They were standing outside the car talking about police matters. My heart began to race at the sight of them. They stopped talking when they saw me. I could feel their eyes on me, while I passed the car. I had the urge to run and hide, but that would make them suspicious, they would follow me like hawks to road kill. I kept as calm as I could until I knew I was out of their sight. Any police officer made me extremely uncomfortable now. I was lucky to be out I really had to count my blessings. I also knew that the cameras were watching me too. I had no choice but to watch my every move.

When I got to the court, Dan and Adrian were playing basketball, while Elizabeth was sitting all by herself on the bleachers. Rather than play basketball, I sat down next to Elizabeth. When she saw me coming up to her, she was in shock.
"Zack are you okay? Dan told me that he saw you getting taken away by the cops this morning"

"Yea, I am okay. I am here right now aren't I?"

"Yes, but what happened?"

"A camera caught me out past curfew last night."

"I'm so sorry! If I didn't mean to keep you out so late."

"Elizabeth don't worry about it, you're safe too. A woman asked me if there was anyone with me. I told her no."

Elizabeth hugged me, she also thanked me for keeping her safe. I am not going to lie, the experience changed me. Even though I had no choice but to accept what had happened, I wanted to change it. I just didn't know how or where to even begin.

After the basketball game, Adrian saw me on the bleachers with Elizabeth. He tapped Dan on the shoulders, while pointing at me. They both ran towards the bleachers, they both sat at the seats below me and Elizabeth. "Dude, are you okay!" Dan shouted. I told him that I was okay I also explained why I got in trouble this morning. I explained in full detail what happened, while I was in the police station. I also told them about the woman who had questioned me. All of them listened to me like I was telling a bone chilling story. In reality, I was telling that kind of story. You never hear about people getting set free, after they get dragged out of their homes by the cops.

"Zack, you are beyond lucky!" Dan said. I laughed, "No I'm not, and if I was lucky I would have never gotten caught. I am not like you Dan." Dan looked at me, he couldn't believe that I even said that. It was the truth though, no matter how many times that he snuck out. He never got caught. I wish I knew the things that he did. I would have been as sneaky as he was, but I wasn't and that's why I got caught. The group just sat there talking about what had happened that morning, for some reason it was the topic of the night. We sat there until it was time for dinner. Dan, Elizabeth, and I walked to the cafeteria. As Elizabeth was walking in, Dan pulled me aside. "Do you want to learn how to sneak out at night, without getting caught?" he asked. I looked at Dan like he was stupid.

"No!"

"You have nothing to worry about I want to show you something tonight. At midnight the person who watches the cameras in our building goes on break. So there is no one watching the cameras, I will be waiting for you at the main doors until 12:15. If you are not there by then, I am leaving without you."

I am a little confused on how Dan knew this information, or where he even got it, in the first place. That is a question that I did not want to even ask him. I walked into the cafeteria, got my food, and met my parents at the table. I was just waiting for Dad to ask me, about this morning. He didn't even ask I think Mom already covered that topic with him. She told him not to even talk about it because it was not the type of conversation that you would want to bring to the table. There was an utter silence during the entire dinner. I liked it, because it allowed me to think about what Dan told me earlier. I was debating with myself if I should even go with him due to the circumstances that took place. I was still wondering on how he knew about the camera system. Only the people in the Government knew about it. Did Dan know someone that monitored the cameras or did he know a Government Official that was corrupted? I would never know, but I really wanted to find out. Right there and then I decided that I am going to risk it. I mean I was already in jail this morning. What else could possibly happen? I would go back, and they would probably set me free again.

After dinner, my parents and I went home. I found my usual spot next to Mom. We watched television until my Dad went to bed. That was also the time that Mom followed and went to bed too. I turned off the television acting like I was going to bed. I just stayed on the couch, starring at my watch, watching the minutes go by until midnight came. I snuck out the door to meet Dan at the building main doors. He was there waiting for me like he said that he was going to be. He had a black hoodie on, when I walked up to him. He handed me a black hoodie, "Here you are going to need this." I grabbed the hoodie out of his hand and put it on. I was a little confused on why I needed it at all. I was here to learn, not to question Dan's tactics. "Follow me" he said.

Dan and I snuck our way a couple of blocks away from the building. He led me to the back of a small office building, he knocked on the back door. "Who is it?" a voice asked, "Dan" he replied. The door opened, Kyle from school was holding the door, letting us in. "What's up Zack?" asked Kyle, "Nothing" I replied. We walked into the building, down a flight of stairs, and into the basement. The room was people filled from adults to teenagers. There were mostly teenagers there, a lot of the people were dressed in dark colors. "Everyone please sit down" a soft voice said. Everyone sat down on chairs in the room, I sat down in the back. Dan was right next to me. A woman walked into the front of the room, to a podium. It was the same woman that was at the police station this morning, what was she doing here? She would be the person that turns everyone in for even being here. There are at least thirty or more people in this room, they should be scared for their lives not listening to a Government Official.

She cleared her voice, before she began to talk. "Thank you everyone for taking the huge risk for being here tonight. For too long we have let this Government take over our lives. We have followed every rule that they have made without question. I, like many of you are tired of living this way." She paused to look at the audience that was before her. "These meetings that we have here are the last freedom that we have left, without the watchful eye of the Government. Soon it will be our time to rise up and destroy this prison that they have built to keep us contained."

I couldn't believe it, someone that actually works for the Government was speaking at secret rebellion meetings. The puzzle pieces came together on why Dan got away with sneaking out at night. The woman knew what times certain cameras were not being watched. "Who is that?" I asked, "That's Katherine, she works for the Police Station and the Government" Dan replied. I knew that she works for the Government, I was just wondering why she was here. I sat there listening to her speech, watching people nod and agree with her. Dan started telling me that she supported a rebellious movement. Also that she was planning a way to destroy the system, and get it back to the way that it used to be. He told me that she idolized Franklin and Teddy Roosevelt. That she was for freedom, freedom of the people along with the entire nation. "I know that things are dim now, my friends but the grass is greener on the other side!" she yelled. The entire room applauded when she was done with her speech.

There was a little whisper amongst the crowd. I couldn't tell if they were moved by the things that she said, or if they were questioning her. I mean she works for the Government, and that does sound iffy within itself. She could have the meeting raided at any point, and have everyone here turned in. I could imagine that would make her look like the shining star amongst her bosses. The idea alone makes my skin crawl, also I'm just waiting for the cops to bust in the doors. But that did not happen, this moment seemed like a dream. It was unreal, I waited until Katherine got off of the stage. Even though there was a swarm of people around her, trying to ask questions on how she was going to pull her plan off. I made myself very present, I got right in front of her and looked her dead in her face "Hello Officer."

Katherine took a minute to remember who I was. "Hello, Zack" she smiled. It was right then that the people around us realized that her attention was no longer on them, it was now on me. They slowly drifted away from us, we started walking around the room.

"I would never expect you here Zack, I thought that the mishap that we had this morning, would scar you for the rest of your life."

"Well, I had a friend that got me here tonight."

"Dan?"

"Yea, he really didn't give me much info about this meeting."

"I am sure that he didn't."

"What is your plan to do anyways?"

"I haven't really thought about it yet, working for the system I know that they hate disorder. That will be the key into my plan. If one person gets out of control, they can handle it. But if the entire nation does it, they will lose control. Thinking about it, what Katherine was saying made perfect sense. The question was how she was going to do it? How could she get everyone to go against the system when everyone fears it? I am the cat and my curiosity will be the death of me.

When the meeting was over, Dan and I made our way home. I was still shocked at what happened tonight. I was still trying to make all the puzzle pieces fit. I felt like a little kid trying to make that one piece fit. Even though it didn't, I'm sitting there banging on it. Forcing it to go where I want, and get mad because the piece is broken due to my own stupidity. When we got to our building, I tried to slowly creep into my house. Mom was sitting on the couch, with her bathrobe on and hate in her eyes. "Where were you?" she screamed, "Out with Dan" I answered. I must have set a fire underneath her because her face turned bright red. "Out with Dan!!!" she yelled. I didn't know what to tell her, or where to begin. If I told her what really happened, I would be imprisoned in my room until the day that I die. So I told her that I was over at Dan's house. That I couldn't sleep and went over to his house. I didn't think that it wouldn't cause any harm because I didn't leave the building. I apologized, trying to make her calm down. Just enough so I can slip my way into my room with less of a guilt trip. It bothered me more that I kept the truth from her, and lied trying to cover it up as best as I could. I was the world's worst liar, lying to mom took guts. My lie let me get away with it, she believed me and told me to go into my room. Which I was more than happy to do.

I slugged into my bed, hoping to fall asleep but my head was way too full to even close my eyes. Plus the fact that my alarm went off in an hour, didn't help either. I felt like a criminal, it felt good. The feeling was mutual to that of a kid talking to Santa Claus on the phone, I love it! There was no surprise that I got up before my alarm went off. The fact that I was already in my school uniform was amazing. I walked into the living room to find my mom sleeping on the couch. She must have been up all night, when she noticed that I was not in my room. I should have known that she would freak out, after what happened earlier. I don't blame her either, if my kid had done what I had done, I would have freaked out too.

I didn't even bother to wake Mom up I just grabbed my backpack and silently went out the door. I found Dan waiting for me at the stairs on my floor. As we were walking down the steps, he whispered "So about last night….." I stopped him, before he could even finish his sentence. "I won't say a word, if that's what you are asking" I whispered back. You could tell that Dan was at ease when I told him this. I mean I didn't even tell Mom, and I tell her everything. We walked our way to the Cafeteria. Waiting in line for breakfast, my mind was still in shambles. I was thinking about all the possible ways that Katherine's plan could work. Would she do it during the day for everybody to see, or at night like the meetings? I really wanted to know what her plan was, it was more like I was dying to know.

Since my mind was a mess, I didn't think about breakfast. So I grabbed at whatever was in my reach, my breakfast consisted of mush that they called oatmeal. Along with the some type of food that they were calling toast, egg mush, and orange juice. I really wasn't looking forward to eating this meal. I knew that I wasn't going to enjoy it at all. With the tray in my hand, I looked for an empty table. Usually Mom eats breakfast with me every morning, it was a rare moment that she didn't. I ended up finding Elizabeth sitting by herself. I sat next to her, she was twirling her fork in the egg mush. "You know it gets a lot easier to eat the food here, if you don't think about it" I murmured. She looked at me and half smiled, "I'm not hungry" she said. I put my hand on top of Elizabeth's hand, since her left hand was resting on the table. "Are you okay?" I asked. She just looked down at her tray, tears started coming down her cheeks. Elizabeth started telling me about how guilty, she felt about the other night. And how bad she felt when she found out that I got dragged out of my house by the cops yesterday morning. I told her that everything is going to be okay, and that it was over and done with. I stopped worrying about it. I actually knew someone that works for the Government, I felt unstoppable.

After breakfast, Elizabeth and I walked to school. It was a rather slow walk but I enjoyed it. I was with Elizabeth and my mind was no longer a mess. For some reason, she made all the troubles go away. They just went "poof!!" like nothing mattered anymore. At school, I couldn't even focus, I almost wore out my three strikes with Mr. Smith. He was even wondering what was wrong with me because I always got his problems completed with the first try. I even got hit in the head with a volleyball in gym. I was completely out of it. After school, I went to the benches like normal, Dan and Elizabeth were sitting there. Dan was watching the basketball game, while Elizabeth was working on her homework. I sat on the bench below them, I laid down on the bench thinking to myself, about the same subject that has been on my mind all day. I stared up at the glass ceiling, wondering what it would be like to be outside. Wondering if I would ever get to go outside, what it even looked like beyond these concrete walls. I felt like a bird wanting to get out of its cage. I would do anything to get out.

"What are you thinking about?" Dan asked. I looked at him with an evil glare. Out of all the questions he could have asked me, he had to ask me that one. He had to know what was going on in my head. Dan had introduced me to an entire new world. The possibilities of that world are endless. There was a bunch of questions that I wanted to ask him the court wasn't the time nor place to do it. Dan backed away, when he saw the face that I was giving him. "Zack, would you like to join me for dinner?" giggled Elizabeth. Before I could even think about it, I said "Yes." I know for a fact that Mom would get mad at me, for not eating dinner with her and Dad. But at the same time, I had already said yes to Elizabeth and I would feel like a fool if I backed out. Plus she likes me, why would she have kissed me the other night? Now she is asking me to eat dinner with her. I would never turn down this opportunity for the world, nobody my age would even dare.

"So let's go, silly!" said Elizabeth. I guess my over thinking made time go slower, than it actually was. I had to snap back into reality just to get my head off of the bench. Yet to get up all together, Elizabeth had her books in her hands. "They look heavy, let me carry them" I said while I extended my hand, reaching for her books. She smiled as she handed me her books, "Are you okay?" she asked. "You don't seem like yourself." I didn't know what to tell her, I wanted to tell her everything. I wanted to show her, but how could I even begin? "I'm fine, I just haven't been getting much sleep lately" I replied. Elizabeth just looked at me, I don't think that she believed me. The expression in her face gave it all away. We got to the Cafeteria, Elizabeth and I got our food, sat down at a small empty table, and slowly ate the food. When I looked up, I could see my parents a few tables away. Mom looked back at me, she just shook her head. Then she looked down at her tray, and continued eating. Dad on the other hand, just smiled. Sometimes I'm happy that my parents are different, Mom worries about everything while Dad doesn't really care. I guess that is the glory of parents.

Neither Elizabeth or myself talked during the entire dinner, we just enjoyed the company of each other. Why bother it with simple talk or we really had nothing to talk about in the first place. After dinner, I walked Elizabeth home. When we got to her building, we stopped at the front doors. When I went to hand Elizabeth her books, she placed her hand on mine, "Would you like to come in?" she asked. I shook my head and smiled. We walked into the building, up the stairs to the fifth floor, and into her home. When we walked thru the door, I saw an old man sitting on the couch. He looked very weak and you could tell that his spirit was broken. "Grandpa, this is Zack. He is the boy that I have been telling you about" Elizabeth said. He looked up at me, the sadness in his eyes made me feel sorry for him. I walked up to him, extended my hand to shake his. "It's nice to meet you sir" I said. "Please, call me John. Calling me sir, makes me feel a lot older than I actually am" he said with a smile. "So you're the one that my dearest Lizzy is talking about?" I shook my head to agree with him but I don't even know what Elizabeth has told her Grandpa about me. The fact that I am a trouble maker would make any parent or grandparent turn away. I'm surprised that I was even allowed in the house, yet alone standing in front of her Grandpa was a shocker.

"So my boy, did you get in trouble for staying out so late, with Lizzy the other night?" John asked. "Yes, I did. I was dragged out of my home and down to the police station that morning" I replied. John started laughing, "This Government is something else. I tell you! I remember a time when the Government wasn't this hard. My father was a war hero, he fought against the Nazis in World War II!" I couldn't believe what I was hearing. I was sitting in front of a direct descendent of a World War II war hero. It was an honor and a privilege. Now it made sense why John was so broken, he was so used to being free and now he has to live like a rat in a cage. That would break anyone's spirit, no matter how strong they are. Elizabeth sat down right next to me on the couch, which was across from her Grandpa. "He does have a lot of stories, don't you Grandpa?" said Elizabeth, he just nodded and laughed. "I bet they never get old!" I laughed, "No! They do not!" John shouted in laughter. Elizabeth turned on the television to the movie channel. "These movies are garbage!" John yelled, "I remember the good movies, the movies that my parents grew up on. The old black and white films." I had never seen a black and white movie in my life before. I had only read about them in history books. Now the movies had to be approved by the Government. John was right, the approved movies did stink. They actually stunk, a lot.

Time flew by while we were watching television. It was nine o'clock before I knew it. "I've got to go home" I whispered in Elizabeth's ear. "Okay" she said, she walked me to her front door, kissed me on the cheek, opened the door, and closed it behind me as I walked out. On my walk home, all I could think about was John. I knew he would be happy to be free again, to not live in this prison called a Dome. When I got home, Mom thankfully was acting somewhat normal. She was watching television she had asked me where I had been, I told her that I was over Elizabeth's house. She didn't even question me about it or why I didn't eat dinner with her and Dad earlier. "Night Mom" I said, she didn't say anything back. Just nodded her head, I walked into my room, got out of my school uniform, into my pair of comfy pajama pants, and crash landed into my bed. My bed was heaven at that moment. I loved my bed, and it loved me.

CHAPTER FIVE

That morning, I was woken up by Mom. She was rapidly shaking me, "Zack wake up!" she screamed. "I'm up!" I yelled back. I was on the floor. I must have fallen off of my bed. I got up, and rubbed my forehead to see if I had any bumps, because my head hurt. It felt like I hit my head on my nightstand when I out of bed. As I took my hand away from my face, there was blood that was on my fingers along with the palm of my hand. I busted my head on the nightstand, it did not feel too good on my head. Thankfully, Mom wasn't in my room or she would have freaked out even more. I walked into the bathroom and cleaned myself up, the best way that I could. It wasn't easy trying to hide it from Mom. I swear she was like a shark, she was able to smell blood from a mile away.

After I cleaned myself up, I slugged my way into the living room. It was Friday, actually the first Friday of the month. This meant no school, because the schools had to send the monthly reports to the

Government. So they could see where the students were at or where they should be. If you were not where the Government wanted you to be, depending on where you are at. You either got held back another year or they would send you to another school, so you could focus on what you were lacking in. I know for a fact that I am above what I should be. I work extremely hard in school.

Today I decided to be lazy, I still had my pajamas on. I really didn't feel like getting out of them either. "Are you going to join me for breakfast?" Mom asked. "No, I'm not really all that hungry" I replied. The truth was, I just wanted to be alone. Even though I hated it sometimes, it brought me peace when I really needed it. When I heard the door close behind Mom, I went to my room and got Dad's iPod. I stashed it under my clothes in my dresser. It was his when he was my age and I am rather shocked that it still works. I put my headphones in, turned it to my favorite song, laid back in my bed, and got lost in the music. It was one of my favorite things to do when I wanted to be lazy, I loved to get lost in music. I laid there for a few hours before I got bored, I could only take it for so long.

I got up and got dressed, I felt like taking a walk. Since there was really nothing else to do, I left Mom a note on the coffee table. Telling her that I was "out and about" and that I'll meet her and Dad at the cafeteria for dinner. I eventually made it out the door and out of the building. To my surprise, Dan was right outside the door talking to a kid, he looked a little older than us. Dan nodded his head and greeted me. "Zack, this is Marcus" Dan said. I nodded my head to greet Marcus, he nodded back. "Tonight" Dan gestured. I knew exactly what that meant, when he said it. It meant that there was another meeting tonight. I had to come up with a plan to get away from my house, also to make up a good story. So Mom didn't have to worry and tell me I could not leave. "Your house?" I asked, "My house" Dan replied. Dan right there gave me the perfect alibi to give Mom why I needed to go out. Dan was having a guy's night at his house, she could not argue. Considering he was in the same building. His mom was really cool too, she would tell any mom that their kid was over there. She really didn't care about anything, she would even let Dan have girls in his room. She even lied to Sarah's mom when Dan was having sex with Sarah in his room. I am the only one outside that circle that knows that Sarah cheated on Jake with Dan. Also that the baby that she is pregnant with is more than likely Dan's. He often told me ways to get away with it in the bedroom without getting caught. I wouldn't dare to even try. Mom wouldn't allow it in the first place. To be honest, I am glad that she wouldn't allow it either.

I walked away from Dan and Marcus, and walked a few blocks thinking what the meeting could be about tonight. "Could Katherine reveal her plan?" I thought to myself. I wondered what the plan would be. I found myself at the doors of Elizabeth's building, wondering if she was even home. I walked into the building, up the stairs, and began knocking on her door. John answered the door, "Hello Zack" he smiled. "Hello" I smiled back. John went to the side of the door and extended his arm to welcome me in. "Elizabeth!" he yelled, Elizabeth didn't even answer. She just walked into the living room, "Grandpa!" she yelled "You could have told me that we had company!" John just laughed, while Elizabeth ran into her room.

Elizabeth was wearing blue shorts with a white tube top. I thought that she looked fine, rather quite attractive. She didn't want me to see her dressed that way. I believe that she was embarrassed that I saw her like that. John had every right to laugh because it was funny. Elizabeth came out of her room with more of a proper outfit on. A pink and blue plaid shirt with acid wash blue jeans. Mom showed me pictures of her when she wore the same type of jeans. You will never see them in the Dome. Elizabeth must have brought them over from England. I'm surprised that they let her keep them, things like that never made it past the checkpoint. "Sorry" Elizabeth said shyly. "What do you have to be sorry for?" I asked, she gave me an evil glare. Like I already know what she should be sorry for, I just wanted to hear her say it.

Elizabeth sat next to me on the couch, "So…" she whispered. "So…what?" I asked

"What brings you here?"

"Well, I…"

"Elizabeth Marie Gordon! Don't be such a silly little girl, the boy here is smitten with you. And he came here to see you!" John interrupted. Elizabeth turned red as a tomato, "GRANDPA!!" she said while gritting her teeth. I chuckled at them both, John was right. I did like Elizabeth, in fact I liked her a lot. "Do you want to go to the park?" I asked. Elizabeth's eyes got big, "Grandpa, can I go to the park with Zack?" she asked. John nodded his head, we both got up and went out the door. When we got to the park, it was full of little kids. The screaming of the kids would drive anyone insane. This was not the place that I wanted to spend time with Elizabeth. "Let's go somewhere else" I told her. She agreed with me, as we were walking I could feel her slip her hand into mine. Our fingers interlocked with each other. This was the deal breaker, I thought that this meant that Elizabeth is now my girlfriend and that I am her boyfriend. There were butterflies in my stomach at the thought of it, we walked a little bit before we found another park. It wasn't with play equipment like the one before, but with benches and what seemed to be endless sidewalks, with flower gardens and trees. We began to walk down one of the sidewalks before it began to rain. Elizabeth began to laugh, "It rains here? How is that possible we are in a closed dome?" "Well my guess it would take forever if you watered parks like these individually, plus all the trees around here. The Government does this once a week so the plants don't die" I laughed. We were drenched. Elizabeth started spinning around with her mouth wide open. Her tongue was out to catch the raindrops and her arms stretched out at her sides. "I thought, I would never see rain again!" she giggled, she was like a little kid in a candy store. "Have you ever kissed in the rain?" she asked, I shook my head "No."

Before Elizabeth, I hadn't kissed anyone besides Mom when I was a kid. Our kiss from the other night was my first kiss. Elizabeth put her hands on my cheeks, got on her tippy toes, and pulled me in for a kiss. The kiss escalated into us making out. I had no idea what I was doing. I tried to follow Elizabeth and what she was doing, but it was difficult because trying to follow someone in making out is nearly impossible. Along with the constant thought of "Am I doing this right" swarmed the brain. Elizabeth grabbed both of my arms and pulled them around her. I got the hint and pulled her closer to me. At the moment I was in heaven and nothing could bring down this mood. Elizabeth smiled at me, "This is true love without the love part" she said. I smiled back at her, was it me or I really didn't know what true love was. All I could tell you is that. It felt right! "So you're mine?" I asked, "Yes!" Elizabeth replied. My spirit lifted even more when I heard her say that.

"Elizabeth, will you come with me tonight?

"To where?"

"It's a secret, just meet me in my building tonight about a half hour before curfew."

"Okay."

I don't know if it was a good idea to invite Elizabeth to the meeting tonight. It was probably a very stupid idea, but I didn't care. Dan would more than likely hate me for it. Right now, I really didn't care. Elizabeth knew what it was like to be free. She wasn't here for long, but she has every right as we do to get the freedom she deserves back. Plus, I figured the more help that we could get, the better off that we are. I just hope Dan is okay with it and doesn't ban me from the meetings.

Elizabeth grabbed my shirt and pulled me to the nearest bench. She turned me around, pushed me to sit on the bench, and sat down next to me. "This is called flirting" she giggled. I looked at her confused, "I could tell that it was your first time making out" she said. "Was I that bad?" I asked, "No! It's not that, I could tell by your body movement that you haven't done it before, that's all" she said. "Thank you god!" I thought to myself. I didn't want to be bad at that, anything but that! I was relieved when she told me that. The rain had stopped, there was nothing but puddles left over. Elizabeth starting jumping in them, laughing while she was doing it. I just sat on the bench, watching her. It was like the Dome wasn't real to her, which is what I liked most about her. Being here didn't bother her. It was like the rain reminded her of home and the memory of freedom. She did not want to let go. I looked down at my watch, it was five thirty and dinner is at six o'clock "Elizabeth, would you like to join me and my parents for dinner?" I asked. "Please call me Liz, I like being called that. Yes I would love to!" she replied.

We walked our way to the Cafeteria, and then we waited in line to get our food. When we finally got it, I looked around the Cafeteria. Until I found the table that my parents were sitting at. I walked to the table slowly wondering if I should tell my parents that Elizabeth is my girlfriend. She followed me, I wondered if she was just as nervous as I was. I sat down at the table, Elizabeth sat right next to me. "Mom, Dad. This is Liz" I introduced her to my parents. "Hello" she said with a smile, "It is very nice to meet you Liz" she said. "What part of England are you from?" Mom asked. "Well, I am originally from here. I was born in Alabama, my parents moved to London when I was a just a couple of months old. They passed a couple of months ago, so now I am living with my Grandpa"

Elizabeth replied. She had cut straight to the point on why she was here, in the first place. "I am sorry to hear that" Dad said. There was a little bit of silence after that, no one knew what to say to break the silence. I mean what could you say, when a girl just tells you that her parents died and she got put in the worst place possible. I mean I have to admit, that this place is better than jail. But I still wouldn't want to be here.

After dinner, I walked Elizabeth back to her building. "Wear something dark for tonight" I told her, "Okay?" she asked with a very confused look on her face. "You will see!" I laughed. We kissed goodbye, Elizabeth went into her building. I made my way to mine, when I got home. Mom played the twenty question game. I told Mom that Elizabeth is my girlfriend and not to freak out because we just started dating. I knew that Mom would freak out anyways. Because Elizabeth is in fact, my first girlfriend. She kept on saying that her baby boy has grown up, while tears began to swell in her eyes. I'm glad that no one was here to see what was transpiring, I would get picked on by everyone including the guys. I did not want that to happen.

After that drama episode, it came down to the business at hand. I had to lie to Mom, so I could get out for the night.

"Mom, can I go over to Dan's tonight?"

"Why?"

"He is having a guy's night over at his house, please can I go?"

"Sure why not."

That was a lot easier than I thought, I still felt guilty about it though. I went into my room and packed my bag. I made sure to pack my black hoodie. When I got done packing, I told Mom goodbye and I went out the door. I reached Dan's door and knocked, Dan's mom answered the door. "Hello Zack" she greeted, "Hello" I greeted back. "Dan is in his room" she said, I thanked her and walked into Dan's room. Dan was sitting on his bed, watching television. "Hey man, I invited Elizabeth to come with us tonight" I told him. "Did you tell her to wear something dark?" he asked, "Yea" I replied. "Good, the more people we have, the better off we are." I was extremely happy that Dan did not get mad at me for inviting Elizabeth. "You thought that I would get mad at you, didn't you?" He asked. I laughed "Yea!"

We both laughed at my stupidity, while we sat there for a bit. Then Dan got up, "Get ready. Its go time." I reached into my bag, grabbed my hoodie, and put it on. Dan got his out of his closet. "Mom, we are going out. We will be back later!" he yelled. "Okay, hun" she yelled back. Dan and I walked out of his house and down to the front doors, Elizabeth was waiting for us. "Okay, girly. You have to keep as quite as you can be and follow me" Dan whispered. Elizabeth got the hint that we were sneaking around outside. You could tell that she was unsure about the entire thing. Me and Dan put our hoods up as we walked outside, Elizabeth was behind Dan. I was behind her. We snuck in the same way that me and Dan had done before. When we got to the building, Dan knocked on the door. We went in, down the stairs, and we were in a room filled with a crowd of people either in dark clothes or black hoodies. "Is this the secret that you were telling me about?" Elizabeth asked, "Yes, this is it" I replied. "What is this place?" she asked, "This is the future" Dan replied. She looked confused, Elizabeth didn't really know what was going on. She didn't really know what Dan meant in the first place. The future could be a lot different things, either good or bad. "Wait and see. It will all come together soon," I told her. "Please everyone take a seat" Katherine said while she stood at the podium. "I cannot thank everyone enough for being here. I know just like every meeting that we have it is a huge risk just being here." She paused

"The other night, I talked to one of you about chaos. From the inside I know that the Government can only control so much of it. They can handle a small group of protestors by force. I'm sorry to admit, but as of right now, we are no match for the system. Considering that they can completely out match us, we would go down like a ton of bricks. Also due to the failure act, when this dome was created. We cannot take that route, if you don't know what the failure act is. It was a bill that was passed to allow the people to take over the Government if it shuts down and the representatives failed to do their job. The people would be allowed to fire such officials as they see fit. I can tell you that the President and congress will do anything they can to make sure that it will never happen. The Government is not flawless, but they hide it well with controlling the people by putting fear in their minds, while teaching each generation to fear the system. My fellow people, the Government is still corrupt in many ways." Katherine took a minute to breath, everything that she was saying made complete and perfect sense.

"It only takes one stone to create a ripple effect in the water, we are that stone. People do think for themselves, even though they will refuse to admit it. That is why we are all here tonight, we are the free thinkers. Now let's get down to business and the real reason that we are here tonight." Katherine started to explain that her plan was to create what she called, "Controlled chaos. We need to create a situation that would break the chains, which the Government has on the people. It would have to happen on a day that the Government couldn't control what was really going on. We would have to create a disturbance around the Dome that would keep the police busy." She explained that due to the cameras that there were only fifty police officers in the entire Dome. Ten higher Officials, such as the FBI and only one person higher than them. "If we could keep them busy all at the same time, we could get away with gaining our freedom back." She also explained that there would be bandanas given to each one of us, to cover our faces as the chaos begins. "I believe in my heart, that this will work. I have studied every corner of the system that I can. With that note my friends, I thank you." Katherine said to the crowd. A lot of the people got out of their chairs and applauded in excitement. Some even whistled, Katherine had brought hope to a once hopeless crowd of people.

"I get it now" Elizabeth smiled, now things made sense to her. "I am all for it!" she said in excitement. All I could do was smile at her. I am more than happy that Elizabeth wanted to be a part of this. I had the feeling that Katherine's speech won her over, or it could be that she wanted to look cool in front of me. It was without a doubt, that it was the speech. "Who was that lady?" she asked, "Her name is Katherine" I replied. "I take it that she works for the Government" said Elizabeth. I explained to Elizabeth that I met Katherine the day that I was taken into the police station. I also explained that I did not know about Katherine's involvement in this. In fact, at the time, I didn't know about any of this. Katherine walked up to Elizabeth and me with a man following her. He had the complexion of a skeleton. "Zack, I would like you to meet Louie" Katherine said. Louie put out his hand to shake mine, "It's nice to meet you Zack." "It's nice to meet you" I said. "Zack, Louie is the head chef in the cafeteria that you go to. He is also my informant" Katherine said. Chefs were also Government Officials considering that the food was a very important factor in the dome. "How many Government Officials are here?" I asked. Katherine smiled, "More than you think." She started pointing people out, "See him?" she asked while pointing out to a small statured man. He looked like an everyday person, "His name is Joseph. He watches the cameras during the day in zone "F"." Katherine paused and pointed out another man. "That's Cliff, he's an officer in zone "M"." Katherine looked around the room. "That women over there, her name is Anna. She is a school teacher in zone "X"."

I couldn't believe that so many Government Officials were here in this meeting. It was rather shocking, "Louie is going to help you and Dan. Since you three are the only ones from Zone "52" that is here tonight" Katherine said. "There's four of us, this is Lizzy. She is from the zone as well" I told her. Elizabeth and Katherine smiled at each other, "You're that girl from England aren't you?" Katherine asked. "Yes, I am" Elizabeth replied. "Don't worry, you'll get your freedom back" Katherine smiled. I started to wonder how Katherine knew that Elizabeth was from England. I mean Elizabeth didn't even say a word. Her accent gave it away instantly, but you couldn't tell if Elizabeth didn't say anything.

"Katherine, how do all these people get here from all these different zones, without getting caught?" I asked. "Well Zack, the people who work on the cameras in the zones, all are a part of this. When I hired them into office to be officials, I chose the people that I went to law school with, I knew that I could trust them. I knew that they want their freedom as much as we do" she replied. "They have learned to hack the footage, so that way if the footage had to be looked over. No one would get caught or in trouble. Plus I've been working as an official for so long that my actions are no longer questioned. I just tell my friends what nights the meetings are and that pretty much takes care of everything." It made the missing puzzle pieces come together, "Plus when I said that the Government was corrupt, I wasn't kidding. There is an Official, a couple of steps on the ladder below the President that has multiple affairs almost every night with a different woman. While his wife sits at home with the children. She thinks that her husband is a good man because he always tells her that he is working late. When the truth is, he's having sex in his office she told me. She also explained that there was another Official that is addicted to cocaine, he gets away with sneaking it in even though drugs were outlawed a long time ago. She also told me about another one that abuses his wife, and a woman that is a ring leader in a sex ring. She pawns off other women to other Officials to do what they please.

I couldn't believe what I was hearing, I didn't want to believe it. I was always taught in school that the Government was in its best form that it has been in years. That they also made a lot of improvements since Obama's term in office. I didn't know about the failure act until tonight. But if the people only knew what was really going on, the people would take over in a heartbeat. "Time to go" Dan said. Both Elizabeth and I agreed, we started walking towards Elizabeth's building. It was six o'clock in the morning, curfew has lifted. So we were free to walk about in the Dome without sneaking around. When we got to Elizabeth's building, I told Dan to go wait outside while I walked Elizabeth in. As we were walking up the stairs to her floor, "How long has this been going on?" she asked. "I don't know. I only found out about it the other night" I replied. I wondered how long it actually was going on, and how was it even possible for Katherine to organize such meetings without getting in trouble herself. When we got to Elizabeth's door, she gave me a kiss goodbye. "Go get some sleep, you look tired" she giggled. I could only laugh back. I was actually really tired and was quite surprised that I haven't passed out due to the lack of sleep. Elizabeth walked inside her home and closed the door behind her, I walked down the stairs and out the building to meet Dan. "So…are you guys dating?" he asked, "Yea, just started as of yesterday" I replied.

"That's good, so are you going to…?"

"Going to…?"

"You know, "do" her?"

"Do what?"

"You know man."

"No I don't."

"Do I have to spell it out for you? Are you going to have sex with her?"

"Dan, I don't know! Is that all you think about?"

"I'm a guy, I can't help it!"

Sex was the last thing that was on my mind right now, in fact it wasn't on my mind at all. Dan and I walked to our building and up to his house. We both collapsed in the living room. Dan was on the couch while I took over the love seat. Dan turned on the television, "Do you boys need anything?" Dan's mom asked. "No thank you, I'm fine" I replied. Dan shook his head no. Dan's mom just walked back into her bedroom. "Dan, how do you know Katherine?" I asked, "She is my half-sister" he replied. When Dan told me that Katherine is his half-sister, I was shocked. Yet it made sense why he got away with so much. He explained to me that his dad was a ruthless teenager, way more than Dan is now. When his dad was our age, he got a girl pregnant. Katherine's mother, Katherine was born in 2006. He stayed with Katherine and her mom until Katherine was about nine. They split up because the relationship was not working out, because they were both way too young. He had to grow up fast. When his dad met his mom, he had just found out that he had lung cancer. Dan believes that it was because of the cancer that his parents got married and had him a couple of years later. Dan lost his dad because of the lung cancer when he was three.

Both Dan and his mom were broken hearted when it happened. Dan being Katherine's younger brother made sense on why his mom didn't care about what he did. Or in fact who he did. You have a family member working for the Government, you could get away with just about anything. Dan took full and complete advantage of it.

We both fell asleep, while watching television. Staying up all night took its toll on me, even though I was hungry. All I really cared about was getting some sleep. Dan's loveseat was not all that comfortable either. I didn't care though, it was a good place to sleep at the moment. Our snoring echoed in Dan's house. We were so tired that our snoring did not bother either of us.

CHAPTER SIX

I woke up from that long needed nap, only to find that the television was off and Dan was gone. His mom was sitting in a chair reading a book, "Where's Dan?" I asked. "He is in his room with some girl" she replied. "God only knows what they are doing in there." I wouldn't dare go in there, to get my stuff. Because I know I would see something that can't be unseen. I couldn't decide, either stay and wait for Dan to get done with whatever he was doing, or leave and come back later, I mean I'm still wearing the same clothes from yesterday. If I went home, Mom would wonder why I was in the same clothes. Then she would figure out that I lied to her, that itself spells out trouble! Right now, I don't even have the strength to deal with the trouble that would bring.

So instead, I found that it would a better idea if I just left and came back for my stuff later. I told Dan's mom that I had a bag in Dan's room and that I would be back later. She told me that she would more than likely be home or if she wasn't, just to walk in anyways because the door would be unlocked. Since Dan keeps on losing his key, and she got tired of replacing it. I had no idea on where to go, Elizabeth was probably sleeping. I did not want to bother her or worse, I might get yelled at by her Grandpa, because she was out all night. I decided to go the Cafeteria to go talk to Louie, that is, if I could talk to him. I walked over to the Cafeteria, it was completely empty. I mean the only time I ever go in it, is when it's time to eat and it's completely packed.

One of the kitchen workers spotted me, "You're not supposed to be in here!" he yelled. "I'm looking for Louie" I told them. "This way" he said while gesturing me to follow him. The worker led me to the back of the kitchen. Louie was there preparing dinner, he was singing to himself while he was stirring something that was in a big pot. "So is that why the food tastes like garbage?" I laughed, "Hey kid, I am working with what they give me to work with" he said. "So what brings you to my place in Hell?" I told Louie that I wanted to see how long he was doing what he was doing. Then he explained that I was free to talk about whatever I wanted to in the kitchen. He explained that there are no cameras in the kitchen, and that all of his staff was at the meeting last night, so I was safe. "How long has this been going on?" I asked. "It's been going on for years, we started as a small group. Slowly generating more and more people" he answered. Then I asked Louie how he got involved, he told me that he is married to Katherine.

"Everything was her idea" he told me, "While her dad was alive, he taught her that America stood for freedom. If you take away freedom there is no America." Louie explained that was the reason why Katherine became a cop, to get in the system and learn how to slowly turn it around or destroy it all together. "Her plan is going to work" he said, I don't doubt that the plan wouldn't work. You could tell by her speech last night that she put a lot of thought into it. "Well kid, I have to get back to work and if you stand there any longer. I will put you to work too!" Louie laughed. I laughed back, I really did not want to work in the kitchen. I would more than likely end up mopping the floors, or worse I would be doing the dishes. I can only see the endless amount of dishes that are at the end of every day. "See you later" I said, "Ditto kid" Louie said back.

When I walked out of the Cafeteria doors, I only had one place in mind that I really wanted to go. That was Elizabeth's house, not to see her though but to see John. I wanted to ask him a few things, I actually had a lot of questions to ask him. While walking to Elizabeth's, I thought of the questions that I wanted to ask John. How to word them too, as I walked into the building. "Well this is it, don't chicken out!" I thought to myself. When I knocked on the door, I took a deep breath. John answered the door, "Hi there Zack, Lizzy is still sleeping. I'll be more than happy to tell her that you stopped by" John said. "No, as much as I would like to see Lizzy right now. I came here to see you" I said.

John had a puzzled look on his face, while he invited me in. He sat down on the couch, I sat down on the chair opposite of him.

"What was it like?"

"What was what like?"

"You know, you growing up. What was it like?"

"Well my boy."

John started telling me stories of his childhood. He told me that he was a part of the baby boomer generation. "You see, after the war, the soldiers came home to their girlfriends or wives and started having lots of kids. I have eight siblings, four girls and four boys. That is nine kids all together" he said. He started telling me about his dad, and how his dad would tell him stories about his time in Germany fighting the Nazis. Then his dad would tell him about the concentration camps. "My dad was only eighteen when he went to Germany, nothing in his life prepared him for what he saw in the camps" John explained. "Only a monster would do such things to people."

I had learned about Hitler in school and about what he did to the Jewish people. John went on to explain that his dad went to Auschwitz, Treblinka, and Balzac. I could only imagine what John's dad saw at the camps. But at the same time, I did not want to picture such a thing in my head. The pictures that I saw at school, put an impression in my mind that I could never forget. John told me about his uncle that died at Pearl Harbor. "I never met my uncle, all though the stories that my dad told me about him. Made me wish that I did. Both he and my father are honorable men, and I am very proud that I am related to them" he said. John explained that his mother helped build airplanes, so she was a part of the Rosie the Riveter women during the war. "I was born on March 16, 1960" John said. He told me that the times were a lot easier than what they are now. "Kids were able to play out in the grass, get dirty, and jump in the lake if they wanted" he said. He explained that kids played as hard as they worked. "Our parents worked, they were only doing what their parents taught them" John said. "That was hard work"

John's eyes started to tear up, "You don't know what you have, until it's gone." I don't think he was talking about the freedom he once had. John missed his family. "My father was my hero, when I was a kid. He still is to this very day, there was no one that could ever measure up to him and my mother. She could bring sunshine into the darkest days" John said. "What about your siblings?" I asked, John began to explain that his older brother, the oldest out of all nine kids died in Vietnam, "He looked up to our father more than I did. He wanted to make him proud by becoming a soldier" John said. "He was based at Bien Hoi, he was killed in action at Saigon in 1975. I was only fifteen when he died, but I wanted to be a soldier just like him." John told me that a couple of his sisters, who were older, volunteered as nurses during the Vietnam War. "When my brother William got drafted, he fled to Canada. Father called him a coward and disowned him," John said. He told me about his other siblings, how his little brother would love to play cowboys with him. "John Wayne was Harding's hero!" John laughed. "Harding? What kind of a name is that?" I asked. "Mother named him after President Warren G. Harding" he answered. "Father wanted all the boys to be named after presidents. There was Benjamin the oldest, he was named after Benjamin Harrison, William, who was named after William McKinley, Theodore, who father proudly named after Theodore Roosevelt, I was named after John Quincy Adams, then there was Harding."

John also said that his father was as American as they come. He expected his boys to do the same. "My sisters on the other hand, were named after famous actresses. Mother always loved the pictures as a kid. There was Claudette, my older sister who was named after Claudette Colbert, the twins, Constance who was named after Constance Bennett, and Corinne, who was named after Corrine Griffith, my little sister Shirley, mother loved Shirley Temple." "I have a lot of research to do!" I laughed, "You don't even know these people that I am naming off do you?" John asked. "The presidents, but not the actresses" I said. "Oh dear boy! You are deprived! My favorite actor is Charlie Chaplin" He said.

"Charlie?" I asked, John looked at me like I was an idiot. "Charlie Chaplin! He was in the "Gold Rush" and "A King in New York" amongst many other wonderful movies!" I felt like a complete idiot, it wasn't even my fault either. School doesn't teach us anything about this, and I didn't even think about asking my parents about these people. "Mother and I went to the pictures to watch a Charlie Chaplin picture, whenever we could" John said. He reached to the table that was next to him, pulled out a drawer, reached in, and pulled out a hat. It was old looking, ragged, with a few holes in it. "Mother made this for me when I was six, she crochet me this hat because the hats that I had, were hand-me-downs from my brothers. Which really didn't do the job during the winters on the farm," he said. John put the memory filled hat back into the drawer. I was shocked that John lived on a farm when he was growing up. John told me about his teenage years and how he met his wife Anna. It was exactly how mine and Elizabeth's relationship started. True love in its purest form. He told me about the greatest moments that he had in his life were the births of his children and becoming a grandfather, "I had a good life before America turned into this" he said. "Hi Zack!" giggled Elizabeth, "Having a good chat with my Grandfather?" she asked. "Why yes, we are Lizzy" John replied. I laughed, "So how long were you sitting there?" I asked. "Sitting? More like standing! Grandfather has told me many stories and how I was named after Elizabeth the Great. The great Queen of England" she giggled.

Elizabeth sat down on the floor next to me. "So are you tired?" she asked. I shook my head no, "You are a horrible liar" she giggled. "Wait what?" I snapped, I couldn't believe it. How did she know that I was lying to her? I mean yes, I am tired but not to the point that I want to pass out. I really did not want to show any weakness. "I could use a nap honestly" I said. A nap? Really I just admitted guilt. Elizabeth laughed at my stupidity, "Would you like to go for a walk?" she asked. "Sure" I replied, "You kids have fun, lord knows what else there is to do around here" John said. Both Elizabeth and I got up from where we were sitting and walked out the door.

We walked around a little bit, talking about all sorts of things. Mostly about her life in England, what it was like to be free. How the grass felt against her skin, the feel of the wind blowing. The smell of the trees in the woods, the sounds of the crickets on a starry summers night and we even talked about the smell of the fresh ground coffee beans in her mother's kitchen. We walked a little bit further until I heard someone call my name, "Zack!"

I heard the voice come from behind me, when I turned around, I turned cold and I felt like my feet were cemented into place. It was Mark, he was the last person that I wanted to see, but this time, he had two of his thugs with him, Jesse and Don. "I have stitches and staples in the back of my head!" Mark said, as he started walking closer, "You will pay for what you have done!" That was something that I did not want to hear, I did not have any walls to shove Mark into this time. He was angry enough that any punch that I threw at him would not even phase him, and for him to call out a fight in the open. That was pure and utter madness.

Fights between enemies are usually hidden deep within the alleyways of the city, where people were lucky not to get caught. Mark came closer, enough to the point that our noses could touch if he got any closer. "You split my head open!" he yelled, "You got what you deserved!" I yelled back. "Zack?" Elizabeth asked in fright, "Well, well, well… who is this pretty little kitten?" Mark asked, "None of your business!" I snapped. "Well the little kitten's hiss is probably worse than her bite. Her purr probably sounds sweeter, don't worry kitten. I'll take care of you" laughed Mark. "You cannot have her!" I snarled, "Then stop me" Mark said. "I am not the one who is picking the fight" I said.

"Sissy!" screamed Mark, while he started pushing me around. "Punch him! The little girl isn't going to do anything!" screamed Jesse. "It's not gym class anymore!" Mark snarled, he pushed me a couple more times before I punched him in the face. Mark's head went back from the impact of my fist, he looked at me in confusion. "Dude your nose" Don said. Mark took his fingers and touched his nose, he freaked out when he saw the blood on his fingertips. "You're dead!" Mark said. Mark started punching me in the face, then in the stomach or where ever his fists felt like landing. When I collapsed to the ground, Jesse and Don joined in. They kept on kicking me and stomping on whatever part of my body they could. I was in the fetal position with my arms shielding my face, "Stop it!" Elizabeth screamed while tears were falling down her face. "Somebody help him!" she screamed "Somebody please help him!"

An officer came running, "I need backup, there's a fight on Wilkinson Street in Zone 54!" The officer pulled Mark off of me, "What the hell is going on here!?" asked the officer. "This boy started a fight with Zack, and these two joined in" Elizabeth replied.

"You witnessed the entire thing Miss?"

"Yes I did, Zack only threw a punch to defend himself."

Two other officers' had shown up, Mark, Jesse, and Don were all in handcuffs. "Zack, is it?" the officer asked, "Yes" I replied. "You need to go the hospital, you are covered in blood" the officer said. He was right, I was covered from head to toe in blood. My clothes were soaked. I didn't feel any pain, at least not yet. It all happened so fast that I really didn't know how much damage that they really had done to me. "Zack, come on. Let's go" said Elizabeth. "We can take you both to the hospital" said the officer. Elizabeth helped me up from the ground and into the police vehicle. I kept on thinking, that I should have gotten a few more punches in during the fight. On the way to the hospital that's all I could think about and I really wish that I did. I mean I wouldn't be the bloody mess that I am right now.

When we got to the hospital, there was a huge crowd in the waiting room. I never knew what went on in the hospitals, since the only time that I was ever in one was when I was a baby. I mean, I went to the regular doctor visits. But I never had to go to the hospital for anything. Mom didn't like hospitals anyways, she said that it was a factory for diseases and it was plagued with the smell of death.

Maybe that was another reason why, that I have never been to a hospital.

I didn't have to wait in the waiting room, they rushed me right into a room. A nurse told me to get a hospital gown on, and to sit on the bed. "I promise, I won't look" Elizabeth giggled. "You better not!" I laughed "Close them!" I waited for Elizabeth to close her eyes and for extra protection, I had her put her hands over them. I started to take off the blood soaked cloths, I noticed Elizabeth peaking at me thru a slit in her flingers. "Hey!" I yelled, "I said no peaking!" she could only start laughing. "Sorry!" she said, I made Elizabeth face the wall before I even thought about getting the rest of my clothes off and getting into the gown. When I sat down on the bed, I told Elizabeth that she could stop facing the wall. "So, why did he do that to you?" she asked, "Mark is a big bully, he always has been. I gave him a taste of his own medicine a few days ago." I replied, "I never thought that it would lead to this."

A knock came from the door, Elizabeth and I looked up. A very small old man slowly walked into the room, his cane led his way. "My name is Doctor Albert, but you can call me Dr. Al" he said in a very sluggishly voice. Dr. Albert looked older than John, his voice trembled like his body. "So, what happened to you?" he asked, "I got in a fight" I replied. "Ah, so you got licked!" he laughed, "licked! That is disgusting!" Elizabeth shrieked. Dr. Albert starting laughing, "Not that kind of licked my dear, it is an old term that my father used when I was a child. It's another word for fight." I looked at Elizabeth like Dr. Albert was insane, whenever I thought of the word licked. I thought of an ice cream cone or a lollipop getting licked and then ate, not fighting. "Well Mister Helenkopf, it seems to me that you have gotten your butt handed to you" Dr. Albert said. "A few x-rays will be taken to make sure that you don't have any broken bones. Then after that checks out, you can take a shower to get off all that dried blood off, we will give you some scrubs to wear when you leave."

"Well, what if I don't have any broken bones?" I asked, "Then you should have some really bad bruising, that's if you are in any pain of course" he replied. "Thank you Dr. Al" Elizabeth said, Dr. Albert smiled at the both of us and walked out the door. It wasn't long before a nurse came in with a wheelchair to take me to the x-ray room. On the way to the room, the nurse asked me what happened. I told her that I got the short stick when it came to facing a bully. "It's very rare that someone comes in here after a fight" she said. "Well, what kind of people, do you usually see that come in here?" I asked, "Mainly, I see people that the government will bring in for evaluation" she replied. "It's mostly women that have lost their minds, because they were told that they are not allowed to have kids" she paused. "I really don't blame them, I would lose my mind if I was told that I wasn't allowed to have kids." I started thinking about what the nurse was telling me. I started to wonder how many women, that have in fact been sent here? How many couples were denied the joys of parenthood? "How many kids do you have?" I asked, "I don't have any yet. My husband and I just got the license to have a child, so hopefully we will have one soon" she replied. She left me at the door to the x-ray room, "Someone will be with you soon. I will be back for you when they are done" she said. I must have waited for only about five minutes at the door, even though it seemed like hours.

When they took some x-rays of my chest, the x-ray technician had me hold my breath and told me to stand as still as possible. The x-ray machine was a huge machine and I really would have liked to know how it worked. I thought about, that if Katherine's plan really worked, I would like to build huge machines when I get older. The bigger the machine, the happier I would be to build it. When they were done with the x-rays, I sat back down into the wheelchair. The technician rolled me out of the door and then told me that the nurse will be here soon to roll me back into my room. The technician shut the door before I could even ask when the results of the x-rays would go to the doctor. The nurse took me back into the room, Elizabeth was fast asleep in the chair. I moved as quietly as possible so I wouldn't wake her. I sat on the bed wondering if I had any broken bones, and if I did. What Dr. Albert would do to fix them? I have never had any broken bones before, so I really didn't know how they fixed them. None of my friends had them either. I thought about it for a while. I started thinking of the possibilities, I wondered if they made you have a surgery. Where they cut you open and fix the bones by putting them in place with metal screws and pins or if you broke something beyond the point that you could not move it. They would put in a computer system that connects to your brain that tells the broken part to move. All of my thinking made the time fly by, the clock on the wall went from three o'clock to six o'clock. It was enough time for Elizabeth to get a good cat nap in, "Any news yet?" she asked. "Not yet" I replied, Elizabeth just shook her head and leaned back further into the chair as much as she could. She attempted to go back to sleep, but she couldn't.

Dr Albert came into the room, "God was looking after you today, my dear boy" he said. "What do you mean?" I asked, "Well son, you don't even have any broken bones. Just a few scratches and some very bad bruises" he replied. I was relieved when he told me that I was okay, I gave a sigh of relief. "There is a shower in the bathroom, here is some scrubs and some soap. After you are done with that you are free to leave, just make sure to check out near the exit" he said. Dr. Albert handed me a pair of black scrubs along with a towel and a small bottle of soap. The soap smelled really gross, but how could I complain? It was a lot better than having dried blood all over me.

After the shower, I got the scrubs on a long with my blood covered shoes. Elizabeth fell back to sleep while I was taking a shower, I woke her up and we made our way out of the door to the check out desk. "Ready to go home?" asked the clerk, "Yea, I am ready for bed" I replied. "Just scan your wrist and you will be all set" he said. As Elizabeth and I walked out, she had a puzzled look on her face, "What's wrong?" I asked. "I don't get it, you go to the hospital and you don't even have to pay. Its like "poof" scan of the wrist and you are free to go. Just like that" she replied. I had to explain to her that since the Health Reform Act that all health care and anything related to health care was free. Doctors were no longer into getting the practice just for the money. They were in it for the good that it had brought to all of mankind in the Dome. A doctor's worth was now measured on how many people he or she helped in their career. Not the size of their paycheck. But it also meant that the other staff, such as nurses, medical aids, desk clerks, and even janitors looked at their jobs as the lowest forms of the medical field. They feel that they could never measure up to the doctors that they work under. It is a never ending tornado of jealousy.

"Well, that's at least one good thing about this place" Elizabeth said, I laughed "There's many good things about this place." Elizabeth looked at me like I was stupid. I told her that our education system has improved greatly since the days that my parents went to school. That jobs were not sent elsewhere because whatever we needed, it was made right here in the Dome. There is no pollution, since there are no cars, that is, if you didn't count the Government cars and even those don't produce pollution. Due to the fact that they are electric and that everything in the dome was free.

I also told her that we pay for these things with our freedom. We as a people, have willingly given up our freedom to have these things. So really, it was a double edged sword. If you actually thought about it. "I never thought about it that way" she said, I shook my head "No one ever does." We ended up walking back to my building, "I'm going to go home" Elizabeth said. We gave our hugs and kisses goodbye before she walked off. Then I walked into the building and up to Dan's to get my bag of stuff out of his room.

CHAPTER SEVEN

As I walked into Dan's house, both he and his mom were watching television. "Sup?" Dan asked, "Nothin' man" I replied "Here to get my bag". Dan nodded his head, then I walked into his bedroom. My bag was on the floor. I grabbed it, and while I was walking out, I said goodbye to Dan and his mom, Dan waved goodbye. When I got to my house, I found both of my parents sleeping on the couch. I am really happy that they are not awake right now, because I really wouldn't know how to even explain why I wasn't at dinner or why I was in scrubs. Instead of my normal clothes. Mom would have a heart attack if she knew that I got into a fight, and the fact that I got beat up would make her die right on the spot. I also know that Dad would not be happy that I didn't hold my own in the fight. He would be ashamed to even call me his son.

As I laid down, I thought about everything that happened. I felt ashamed that Elizabeth had to see me get beaten up so badly, was I really that much of a sissy? Do I even dare try to pull off the tough guy act in front of her? I mean, I am only fifteen. Should I even be wondering about such things? All this over thinking is going to keep me awake, I needed to sleep. I have school in the morning and I dread on missing days because of my over thinking.

I eventually went to sleep, I got woken up by a bad dream. I found myself screaming at the top of my lungs. I had never had a dream that had woke me up before. In fact, I really never had any nightmares. Besides when I was a kid, they were mainly about the monsters under my bed, or the boogey man that stayed in my closet. But this was different, it seemed so real. The dream started out like any other, it actually started like my everyday life. I woke up to my alarm clock going off and got ready for school, even the school day was normal. At the end of the day, Dan told me that Katherine wanted to have everyone that goes to the meetings to meet her by the main Government building in Zone 36. That it was time, time to regain our freedom. I went and got Elizabeth so she could go with us, when we got to the building. There was a huge crowd, bigger then what there originally was at the meetings.

Katherine was standing on the steps that led to the front door, "It is time to create chaos!" she screamed. Then everyone started to spread into a tornado of madness. Breaking the windows of several buildings, they destroyed everything that was in their way. The people that were in the streets, hid where ever they could. If they couldn't hide, they were beaten up by the monstrous people that said that they were doing it for freedom. Then when the police showed up, they started beating down everyone with a club. No matter if they were a part of this madness or not. People started to retaliate against the police, stealing the clubs and beating the police back. I just stood there, and watched. Elizabeth stood right next to me, crying and screaming for this madness to stop. The sound of shots being fired started ringing in my ears, it was guns. How could it be guns? I thought that they didn't exist anymore.

Elizabeth crotched down with her hands on her stomach, her hands were covered in blood when she lifted them. She had been shot, there was a blank look on her face when she looked up at me. That blank look instantly turned, into a terrifying and scared expression. Elizabeth lifted up her shirt, to see where exactly she had been shot at. There was a bullet hole right next to her belly button, blood was pouring out of the wound. She began to scream, while putting her hands over her stomach. Dan came running over to see why Elizabeth was screaming. While he was standing before us. Then he arched his back, like someone hit him on his back a little too hard.

Dan suddenly sounded like he was choking, gasping for air. He looked scared, his shirt was covered in blood. Then started coming out of his mouth. He collapsed to the ground, Dan was shot in the back. The bullet had pierced his lungs, and exited out of his chest. He laid there dead before Elizabeth and me, the sight made her freak out even more. I told her to lay down and that everything would be okay. When the truth was, I didn't know how everything would end. I sat down behind her, cradling her in my arms. Telling her to please hold on, begging Elizabeth not to leave me. We laid there for a little bit, while she was slowing dying in my arms.

That's when I woke up from the nightmare, that's when I woke up screaming. I could only hope that it would not end up like that, because if it was then I wanted nothing to do with it, I didn't want anyone to get killed. Unnatural death is not welcome in my life, if losing a life is what it takes to get back freedom. Then it's not worth it, I'd rather keep the miserable life that I have, even if it means that I can grow old. And live to my full potential. I sat there on my bed for a little bit, trying to get myself together. I grabbed my bag from the floor, opened it, and I saw a piece of paper in it. Dan must have put the paper in my bag while I was out with Elizabeth. I unfolded the piece of paper, and it said "Tonight." I hope Dan meant tonight and not last night, because if it was last night. Then I had missed a meeting that Katherine would explain her plan at.

After getting ready for school, I walked down to the Cafeteria with Mom. "So you're going to wear your school uniform to Sunday school?" she asked. "Is it Sunday?" I replied, Mom laughed. Sunday school wasn't typical Sunday school where the church was involved. This Sunday school was actually school, students had the option to go. If they didn't go, it didn't count against them. You didn't have to wear the school uniform either, you could just show up in everyday clothes. It wasn't the typical school day either, you didn't have classes. There were tutors to help you with any subject that you had problems in.

I just went every other Sunday, to make Mom happy. I would do my homework, or the tutors would allow me to help the younger kids. The tutors were teachers that had nothing better to do, or they loved teaching that much. They wanted to teach kids twenty four seven. Sometimes I would see Adrian there because he really needed the help with math. I guess he got tired of staying after school, with the dreaded Mr. Smith. I would often help him even though we would sit there and joke around more than anything. After breakfast, I was walking to the school when an Officer stopped me. "You Zack Helenkopf?" he asked

"Yes sir."

"I need you to come with me."

"Why?"

"I need you to explain, what events led up to yesterday."

I looked at the Officer confused. Then he told me that I wasn't in trouble, and that I had nothing to worry about I opened the back door to the car and got in. The Officer drove down to the police station. When we entered the garage. I started thinking about what Mark possibly could have told them. I wondered if he told them that I shoved him into the wall, and that it was my fault that his head was split open. Though it would not justify that he beat me to a bloody pulp. The Officer parked the car and got out, then he led me inside the building to a room with a table and two chairs. "Take a seat" he said, then he closed the door behind him.

I sat there waiting a little bit, before I heard someone grab the door handle and began to twist it to open the door. It was Katherine, "Hello Mr. Helenkopf. It seems that you got into some trouble yesterday" she said.

"Yes I did."

"I'm surprised that it wasn't you causing the trouble."

"What is that supposed to mean?"

"Well, after the last time that you were in here. I'd figured that you would never want to come back."

"Trust me, this is the last place that I would ever want to come back to."

"So, do you mind telling me what happened? What exactly led Mark to beating you up yesterday?"

I started telling Katherine about what happened during gym class, I told her that the class started like any other, That the teacher thought that it would be a good day to play basketball. The game got a little rough when the boys were playing the game. I explained that I had the ball, then Mark was trying to take the ball away from me. That he was in between the wall and me. "I was pushed, and I collided into Mark. That's when he hit the wall" I said. "It all happened so fast, I really don't know how it all happened." "So, Mark thinks that you pushed him into the wall on purpose?" Katherine asked. "I guess so, I would never hurt anyone in that manner" I replied. "You are free to go" Katherine said.

Katherine must have known that I was lying to her, about everything. I just can't believe that I got away with it. I missed Sunday school too, Mom usually waits for me because Sunday is the day that our family spends time together. We usually play games or let Dad and Mom share stories about when they were growing up. I just hope that I could beat Mom to the school, so she doesn't know that I wasn't there in the first place. I ran to the school, which thankfully wasn't too far from the police station.

I reached the doors before Mom, had even showed up. I waited on the bench that was near the doors, Mom walked up to me "How was school?" she asked. "Okay" I replied, all I could think about was for her not to ask me about what I had done for the day. I didn't know what to tell her I didn't have any homework and I had no left over school work from the week. Would I tell her that I helped the younger kids with their work? Or do I just leave it at "Okay." That would open up a lot of questions, I would have to come up with more lies. When we got home, Mom asked me to sit down on the on the couch. "Zack, is there anything that I should know about?" she asked. "Oh no!" I said inside my head, those are the words that no kid wants to hear. Whenever I heard it from Mom, it meant that I didn't do a good job of hiding something. Or she heard something from the grapevine from the other moms in the building. I mean, I really didn't start that much trouble. It was usually some things that me and the guys usually talked about. That the other moms would secretly listen to. Dan's topic was always sex, I would get in trouble for what Dan talked about. Because Mom thought that it was always me.

Did she find the note that Dan left in my bag? That was a ticking time bomb if she found it. Trying to be sly, I told her no. "Then what are these Zack!" she said angrily while holding up the scrubs, that I got from the hospital when I was released. I was relieved that she didn't find the note, but explaining what had happened was going to be a doozy of a story to tell. I explained to her that I got beaten up by Mark from school, and a couple of his thugs. "I didn't tell you Mom, because I didn't want you to worry" I said. "Me worry? Zack come on" she said, I gave Mom a strange look. She's a mom and all moms worry about their kids. With the events that have been going on, I don't blame her for worrying at all. She would have a heart attack if she really knew what was going on. Only time will tell what would happen when she finds out.

"Can I go over Dan's tonight?"

"On a school night?"

"Yea, I mean we are in the same building."

"I know"

"Mom, I promise I will meet you for breakfast."

"Zack, you really promise?"

"Yes Mom, I promise."

"Okay, Zack you can go."

After I got the okay to go to Dan's, I packed my messenger bag with my school uniform and I put on a pair of jeans and my black hoodie, Instead of going over to Dan's, I went to Elizabeth's house. She was quite surprised to find me at her door. "I thought that you'd be resting today" she said. "There's a meeting tonight" I told her. "Is that Zack?" John said in the background. "Yes, Grandpa" Elizabeth said, "Well invite him in, Lizzy!" he laughed. I walked in thru the door. Elizabeth sat down on the couch, she didn't look too happy. In fact I don't think that she was even happy, to see me. All of a sudden John started coughing, so much that he began gasping for air.

Elizabeth got up and got an oxygen mask that was on the floor near his feet. "Here you go Grandpa" she said. "Thank you darlin" he smiled. "Grandpa, you should go lay down and get some rest" she ordered, "Zack, can you help him please?" I shook my head and helped John to his bed. When I got back into the living room, I found Elizabeth crying. "What's wrong?" I asked, "He is dying" she replied. Elizabeth told me that the doctors told her that John has cancer, and that is so far along that they can't do anything about it. The President might have found the cure to every known cancer to man, but the biggest down fall is that the cancer has to be treated in the first stages. People still died of cancer, but that's because they either caught in to late or they didn't get treated at all. Who knows how long, John was dealing with this before he told anyone. John had asked Elizabeth to live out their lives as normal as possible. "He's all I have left, I don't know what I would do without him" she wept. "Zack he needs to be free."

I agreed with Elizabeth, John was born free and he should die free. Right then, I made it my goal to do whatever Katherine wanted me to do, in her plan for us to be free. Not only for Elizabeth, but for John too. No one should ever end their life caged up like an animal. I began to debate if should tell Elizabeth about the dream that I had. I wondered if it would be a good idea or not, I decided that it would not be a good idea because it might scare her to the point that she wouldn't want to go to the meeting tonight. The last thing that I would want to do, is to scare her.

We both laid on the couch waiting for time to pass, so we could go. John came out of his room, "Zack my boy. So what is this meeting that you were talking about?" he asked. "I mean you did say it at the door, didn't you?" I didn't know how to explain it due to the microphones and the cameras. I really didn't know who was listening at the time, "Just a bunch of us kids, are talking about getting a basketball team up and running." John shook his head "Back in my day, it was baseball." I laughed "What's baseball?" I asked, "What is baseball!" John screamed. "Only the greatest past time in American history!" John paused while he put the palm of his hand on his forehead. "What's baseball, lord what do they teach you guys in school?"

John started telling me about baseball. He told me about this guy named Babe Ruth. John called him The Great Bambino and how he was an amazing baseball player. He also told me about another guy named Mickey Mantle and another guy named Joe DiMaggio. "Father was a huge fan of the New York Yankees" John said, "There was this guy named Arnold Rothstein. Who they thought that fixed the World Series in 1919" he laughed. "Who is he?" I asked, "Oh boy!" Elizabeth laughed. John looked at me like I was dumb founded. "They don't teach you anything in that crappy school that you guys go to!" he said, "Gangsters boy, gangsters! During prohibition, you know about that don't you?" I shook my head yes, I did learn about it in school that the 18th amendment was created to prohibit the manufacture, sale, and transportation of alcohol in the United States. But we never learned about the people that took part in it, John told me about Arnold Rothstein. He was the leader of the Jewish Mob in New York. Then he told me about Lucky Luciano, "Charlie "Lucky" Luciano worked for Rothstein" John said. He mentioned a guy named Al Capone, "Capone was a good and bad man at the same time" he said. "He was mentored by Giovanni "Johnny" Torrio at the time before Capone went to jail. Capone loved his mentor so much, he had guards monitoring Torrio while he was in the hospital. After a failed assassination attempt on Torrio's life."

John had many stories to tell me about baseball and gangsters. I felt like I could listen to him forever. I loved the fact that he knew so much, and I felt ashamed that I knew so little. There was proof that the schools didn't really teach us anything. You would think that they would go into strict detail about what happened in American history. I mean this seemed like pretty important history, why weren't they teaching it in the schools? History is taught so that way it wouldn't be bound to repeat itself. Since we know too little, I wouldn't doubt that history would repeat itself with my generation. Maybe they didn't teach us it because they thought that it would give us ideas on how to get free, and they wouldn't want that either way.

"Grandpa, I would love to hear your stories but we got to go" Elizabeth said. "Really?" I asked, "Yes silly!" she replied. I was quite sad that it was already time to go, I wanted to hear more of John's stories, about the old times, along with the people in it. As we were walking towards the meeting building, Elizabeth paused "I'm sorry about my Grandpa, he does get carried away sometimes" she said. "Please, I love his stories! I love history" I laughed, "He is actually quite interesting" we began to walk some more.

"Zack?"

"Yes?"

"Do you believe in true love?"

"Do you?"

"I don't know, Grandpa talked about it like it's the greatest thing in the world, I just don't know sometimes."

"Well, why do you say that?"

"I don't know, I'm just crazy I guess."

"Everyone's mad, Elizabeth."

I grabbed her by her hands and pulled her close, "Elizabeth, I am in love with you" I confessed. I expected her to run away from me as fast as she could, but instead her eyes lit up like a Christmas tree. "Zack, I love you" she whispered, she took her hands away from mine and wrapped them around me "True love is real" she laughed.

After we had our little love moment, we continued our way to the meeting. When we reached the building, I knocked on the door. Only to be complicated with a new person at the door, "Who are you?" he asked. "I'm Zack" I said, "Zack who?" he asked. "He is with me!" Dan answered, "Oh, sorry Dan!" he whimpered. "What are you doing answering the door?" Dan asked. "Kyle is using the bathroom, he asked me to watch after the door" he answered. "Don't be stupid next time, you know that Zack comes here. You have seen him here many times!" Dan growled. He just nodded their head like a soldier taking orders from their captain.

We all walked down the stairs into the room, everyone was sitting in their seats waiting for the meeting to start. I have never seen it so still before, until Katherine spoke in front of them. There was usually a huge noise until Katherine took the stage, were they even wondering what her plan was? Did they even have any questions, thoughts, or concerns? I had a boatload of questions that I wanted to ask, I just didn't know what to ask first. Most of all, I wanted to tell Katherine about my dream, and to hope that everything doesn't go the way that it did in my dream.

Everyone stared Katherine down as she stood in front of the podium, "My friends before we get down to business, I would like to recite a speech from *The Great Dictator"* she paused clearing her throat. "In the movie, Charlie Chaplin says this, "I'm sorry, but I don't want to be emperor. That's not my business, I don't want to rule or conquer anyone. I should like to help everyone. If possible

Jew, Gentile, Black Man, White Man. We all want to help one another. Human beings are like that, we want to live by each other's happiness, not each other's misery. We don't want to hate and despise one another. In this world there is room for everyone. And the good earth is rich and can provide for everyone. The way of life can be free and beautiful, but we have lost the way.

Greed has poisoned men's souls, has barricaded the world with hate, has goose stepped us into misery and bloodshed. We have developed speed, but we have shut ourselves in. Machinery that gives abundance has left us in want. Our knowledge has made us cynical. Our cleverness, hard and unkind. We think too much and feel too little. More than machinery we need humanity more than cleverness, we need kindness and gentleness. Without these qualities, life will be violent and all will be lost. The aeroplane and the radio have brought us closer together. The very nature of these inventions cries out for the goodness in men, cries out for universal brotherhood, for the unity of us all. Even now my voice is reaching millions throughout the world, millions of despairing men, women, and little children. Victims of a system that makes men torture and imprison innocent people.

To those who can hear me, I say do not despair. The misery that is now upon us is but the passing of greed, the bitterness of men who fear the way of human progress. The hate of men will pass and dictators die, and the power that they took from the people will return to the people. And so long as men die, liberty will never parish. Soldiers don't give yourselves to brutes, men who despise you, enslave you, who regiment your lives, tell you what to do, what to think, and what to feel. Who drill at you, diet you treat you like cattle, use you as cannon fodder. Don't give yourselves to these unnatural men, machine men with machine minds and machine hearts. You are not machines! You are not cattle! You are men, you have the love of humanity in your hearts. You don't hate! Only the unloved hate! The unloved and unnatural. Soldiers don't fight for slavery, fight for liberty.

In the 17th chapter of St. Luke it is written. "The kingdom of God is within men" not one man nor a group of men. But in all men, in you! You, the people have the power. The power to create machines. The power to create happiness, you the people have the power to make this life free and beautiful, to make this life a wonderful adventure. Then in the name of democracy let us use that power. Let us all unite, let us fight for a new world, a decent world that will give men the chance to work, that will give youth a future and old age a security. By the promise of these things, brutes have risen to power. But they lie! They do not fulfill that promise, they never will! Dictators free themselves but they enslave the people! Now let us fight to fulfill that promise. Let us fight to free the world, to do away with natural barriers. To do away with greed, with hate and intolerance. Let us fight for a world of reason, a world where science and progress will lead to all men's happiness. Soldiers in the name of democracy let us all unite!'"

A roar of applause echoed in the room. Never in my life have I ever heard such words, and the truth behind them. Katherine thanked the crowd and told us that it was because of that speech that she became what she is today. Who knew that a speech that was written before the time that someone was born, could have such an impact on their life? It made an impact on mine, "As I told you before, its chaos. Chaos is our only key, the police have no choice but to answer any call that they receive" Katherine said. She began to explain the plan was to create just enough chaos, so that way the police would be busy with any minor thing that would be going on. While holes were being blown in the wall. Since there was no buildings near the walls of the Dome, people never hung around the walls. If they did they would get in trouble anyway, she estimated that it would take about six bombs in six different spots, to create enough holes for people to get out. "One hole they can secure, six different holes with people rushing out will be an issue for them" she said. "It's us against them." She told us that she will pick the areas to place the bombs and the people who will create them. They would have to make the bombs in the meeting room, because in the home would be way too risky. She would also hand pick the people that would create the chaos and how they would do it. "It would take some times for this to work. I expect us to be free in two day's time. So be ready!" Katherine said.

More applause echoed the room when she walked off the stage. I couldn't believe it, the plan seemed so simple and yet so hard and complicated. Katherine didn't give the people the opportunity to ask questions while she was on the stage, she just wanted to get the business over and done with, she said what she had to say and after that she was done. I rushed to the stage before she could even reach the first step. "Hey Zack, you look worried, what's wrong?" she asked, "I had a dream" I replied. Katherine looked at me a little confused. "A dream?" she asked

"About?"

"Your plan…everything ended in chaos, Elizabeth and Dan were killed."

"Zack, I can promise you that nothing like that will happen. I'm not going to have anyone get hurt or even killed."

"Then how are we going to create this distraction?"

Katherine explained to me that violence was not an option in gaining our freedom back. She told me that even when a student creates a little distraction in class such as a paper ball getting tossed around in class. That the cops had to be called, because that is a sign of a free thinker and a possible danger to the Dome and the control of the Government that it has on it. "Remember Zack, one stone can create a hundred ripples in the water" Katherine said.

Katherine also explained that it would take a couple of days to make the bombs and with her job it would be hard to make them during the day. "We are not the only ones having these meetings Zack. There are about ten groups of us in the Dome. I am just the ring leader in this circus" she laughed. "Most of the groups are led by Government Officials and people that I work with. I have discussed my plan with them, they also think that this is a good idea. We plan on putting at least sixty holes in the dome, so people can get out."

This within itself put my mind at peace. "Zack, on Tuesday start disturbing class at nine on the dot" Katherine said. I smiled, the taste of freedom was so close but yet so far. The child inside of me was screaming and jumping at the same time. I just wanted to start dancing, but embarrassment kept me from doing so. I just danced inside of my head, and it was such a glorious dance.

It was about four in the morning, when the meeting had ended. The room was cleared. But I stayed. I was too excited to sleep and I got permission from Katherine to allow me to stay in the room until six. I played around on the stage. I acted like there was a crowd of people before as I stood at the podium. Ready to make my acceptance speech as President. "President Helenkopf" I thought to myself, "Yea that sounds perfect!" I laughed at myself for such an idea. A person has every right to dream and no one could ever take that away from them. As I stood there, I started talking in a deep big voice. "My first act as President of this free nation, is to reward every free thinker out there!" I waved my hands around like every President did in the videos that I saw at school. As I walked away from the podium, I imagined the crowd applauding and cheering at my pretend speech. I laid down on the edge of the stage, half of my legs dangling off of the edge. I began to think about what it would be like to be free. I wondered what it was like on the outside, was it the wasteland that the Government told us that it is, or would it be new. Everything rebuilding itself without humanity destroying its progress. I was dying to know.

CHAPTER EIGHT

When I looked at my watch it was a quarter to six, I had to hurry to get my school uniform on. I knew Mom would never let me hear the end of it if I didn't meet her for breakfast. I rushed out of the room, up the stairs, and out of the building. I ran to the Cafeteria hoping that Mom was still there. I was glad to see her sitting at the table that we usually sat at. I quickly got my food, and rushed over to the table.

"I'm sorry that I'm late Mom."

"Have fun last night?"

"Yes, Mom I had fun."

"Well what did you guys do?"

"Guy stuff Mom."

Mom gave me the look that she gave me when she usually tried to dig deeper to get the answer out of me. This time, that was not going to work. I was not going to cave in, no matter how hard she tried to dig her way in.

After breakfast, I walked to school. When I got there, a big crowd was at the basketball court. I made my way to the center of the crowd, Dan and Jake were in the center. Jake was screaming at Dan. Jake had found out that Dan was sleeping with Sarah, whenever they weren't together. "Sarah told me that she is pregnant with your baby!" Jake screamed. "How could you do that to me man, you are my family!" that was the first time that anyone found out that Dan and Jake were related. "Water is thicker than blood dude, where were you when me and my mom were going thru hard times?" Dan yelled back, "You were never there!" That just heated up Jake even more, "It doesn't mean that you have to sleep with my girlfriend Dan, that's messed up!" "She doesn't even love you! I don't know why she is with you in the first place" Dan yelled. "You're never there for her and you cheat on her left and right." A few years ago, Dan's mom hit rock bottom. It was a few of years after his dad had passed. His mom couldn't take it anymore and tried to commit suicide by swallowing a bottle of pills that was in the bathroom. She was sent to the hospital, Dan lived with me and my family for a couple of months until she got out. But Jake was right, that didn't give Dan the excuse to do what he had done.

The school principal came out of the school to break up the crowd. "Do we have a problem here?" he asked, "No sir" Jake answered. "Mrs. Arden is about to call the police, I think it's about time for everyone to get to class" Mr. Anderson said. So everyone went into the building and to their classes. The police didn't need to be called, not yet, Mr. Anderson knew that as much as I did. He didn't know it, but I saw him at last night's meeting. Plus a couple of meetings before that. Calling the police was the last resort, plus the fact that it wasn't time yet was another factor into this big dilemma.

I slugged into Mrs. Keen's class, the day had already started out bad and the fact that I haven't slept yet, made me not want to be there anymore. I just wanted to go to bed, "Good morning everyone. I hope you all had a good weekend" she said. "Instead of having a normal class today, we are all going to watch the President during his press release on television today." Mrs. Keen pulled down the projector screen, turned off the lights, and turned on the projector. There was a new announcer on the screen. "This is Janet Bronsen at the White House. We are waiting for the President to come on stage for this morning's press release" she paused. "Sources have told me that he has some very important topics to discuss with us on this wonderful morning" Janet said. The camera went off of her onto the stage that the President usually made his speeches. He walked out of the doors, onto the stage and stood by the White House podium before the ocean of people and cameras.

"My fellow Americans, I work endlessly to ensure your safety along with the safety of this nation. As of today, our borders to other countries are going to be shut down and they are going to remain that way until myself and Congress see fit. Also any non American citizens will be deported back to their country within a few months' time" he said. My ears began to ring, that could possibly mean that I could lose Elizabeth. Since she is from England, she could be deported back there. The numbers didn't grant citizenship to the Dome, it just meant that you lived here and followed protocol. The only way people got true citizenship, was a piece of paper that was issued by the Government. And even though Elizabeth was born here, she moved before the Dome was created so that wouldn't count either. I watched the President as he continued his speech, "To keep our nation safe the curfew is now eight o'clock instead of ten o'clock" he said.

"Really? What more is he going to take away from us?" I thought to myself. "And on another note, the marriage proposal has now been passed into law" the President said. The marriage proposal act was an act that allowed the Government to say if you are allowed to marry or not. It didn't matter to who you wanted to marry. It plainly states that you were not allowed to get married period.

At that point, I just shut the President and his ignorance out. The Government was taking more away from the people, more of the little freedom that they had and the saddest part was the people accepted this. Was the Government's main goal to bleed the people dry? If so then they had already started the process. I laid my head down on my desk wishing that all this would just go away.

In the corner of my eye, I could see Mrs. Keen crying at her desk silently, as the tears rolled down her face. It was hitting her hard, more than the rest of us in the class. I didn't know why she was crying in the first place, but whatever it was. It hit home, because she was a very joyful person even on the bitterest of days. I waited until the speech of insanity was over and Mrs. Keen turned off the projector. I walked up to her desk. "What's wrong Mrs. K?" I asked, "My daughter can't get married to her boyfriend now. He asked her to marry him two months ago, they have been planning their wedding ever since" she replied.

"Why can't they get married?"

"She's bipolar, we heard about that Act but me and my husband thought that it wouldn't pass."

"Don't worry Mrs. K, everything will be okay."

I couldn't believe what I was hearing. I never really got into much detail of the Act because marriage was not in my future any time soon, but now they could deny someone the right to get married because of a condition that they have. It was wrong on so many levels. I tried to comfort Mrs. Keen as best as I could, but it wasn't working. I wish that I could tell her that freedom was only a day away and that her daughter could marry who ever she pleases. No matter if she is bipolar or not.

The bell had rung, I decided to stay with Mrs. Keen until I knew that she was going to be okay to teach her next class. I didn't care if I was going to be late to Mr. Smith's class or not. My heart would not let me, leave even if wanted to or not. Mrs. Keen wrote me a note that excused me for being tardy to class. Then she gave me a hug and thanked me for being there for her. She is a good teacher and a good person. The last thing that I ever wanted to do, was to see her cry. I couldn't stomach that either.

When I got to Mr. Smith's class, I tried to be as quiet as possible. Which that couldn't be done because Mr. Smith could hear a small pitter patter of a single mouse. "Mr. Helenkopf, why are you late?" he asked. I didn't say a word. I just handed him the note that I had received from Mrs. Keen. "Take your seat!" he snarled, I didn't think that he was too happy that I was excused from being late from his class. As I sat down, he pointed to the problems that were on the bored. "Ugh!!" I thought to myself, the last thing that I wanted to do right now was to do math problems. I had too much going on in my head already and math was on the very bottom of my thinking list.

Adrian was sitting next to me, twirling his pen around the paper. "You know, if you twirled that fast enough, I bet you could make it dance!" I laughed. Adrian looked at me funny, "The pen?" I said. "Oh, I wasn't even thinking about that" he said, "Could you believe that Dan got Sarah pregnant? Also that Dan and Jake are related?" Adrian whispered, "I knew that Sarah and Dan were doing it!" Annie said. "Well duh, I mean you are Sarah's best friend Annie" I said, "Who invited you into this conversation? But out!" Annie was the type of girl that loved to get into everyone's business, then later gossiped about it to everyone under the sun. The only person's secrets that she kept was Sarah's, because their friendship was the only one that she could ever keep for this long. Annie is beyond annoying, I am rather surprised that Sarah is even friends with her. Annie just squinted her eyes and shriveled up her nose at me. The only part that she had left out was her sticking out her tongue, then that would have been the completely childish face that she had so much desired to give me.

"I wish people would stay out of our conversations" I said, "Agreed!" Adrian laughed. "Boys! Get back to work!" yelled Mr. Smith. That was the cue to stop talking and also to focus more on the school work. I did my math work as fast as I could. As I walked up to Mr. Smith's desk, I started to wonder if I did my work as best as I could. I wondered if I would get sent back to my desk and have to do it all over again. I took a deep breath as I handed Mr. Smith my paper, my skin began to crawl as I watched him look it over. "Very good Zack, but I don't ever want to hear you talk in this class during work time ever again" he said. "Yes sir" I respectfully said, my heart started beating again. When I knew that I didn't have to go back to my desk with a paper in my hand, I sat right back down into my chair, I put my arms on my desk in a circle form. I laid my head right in the middle. I waited for the bell to ring, so I could go to my next class. I really wanted to go to gym class, I could get some anger out while playing a sport.

The bell rang and I rushed to the locker room. The quicker that I could get into my gym uniform, the quicker that I could get it on. The quicker that I could get on the gym floor. I was the only one there so far. I mean, I did rush to get there. Slowly my other classmates made their way into the gym. Mr. Clyde was sitting in his chair right next to the gym wall, he waited until a few more people showed up before he decided to tell us what he wanted us to do for the day. "It's a free day today, so go have fun!" Mr. Clyde said. My favorite part of gym class was a free day we were allowed to do anything that we wanted. Any sport or just walk around the gym if that is what we really wanted to. The girls would usually just walk around the gym and gossip about girl things, some of the guys wanted to go into the weight room and work out. Me, I just grabbed a basketball. I would just shoot it in baskets, just to do it. I would sometimes count how many baskets I made in a row. If I missed, I would restart all over again. I did that for the entire gym class until Mr. Clyde told us that it was time to go back into the locker rooms.

Lunch time was a little abnormal, the group was rather silent. I don't know if they really had nothing to talk about or if they had a lot on their minds like I did. Dan had broken the silence "So that speech this morning…" he said. "What about it?" I asked, "What about it!" he snarled "That new Act ensures that I will never get married!" I looked at Dan confused, "What?" I said. "Yes man! I cannot get married!" he said. "Why?" Elizabeth asked, "My dad" he answered. Everyone looked at Dan like he was crazy, he told us that story about how great his dad was many times before. But he never had told us the story that he began to tell us at the table, "My dad was a part of the protesting when the Dome was first created" he said. "He got caught and spent some time in jail, the only reasons that he got let out was because me and my sister needed our father in our lives." Dan's mom was still pregnant with him, when the last group of people moved into the Dome. He is a part of the first generation that was ever born inside of the Dome. I used to joke around with him and call him "Dome born." He would get mad about it every time, "I spent the first couple of years of my life without my dad. Even though he missed out on so much, he made up for it when he got out" Dan paused. "Now me and my sister have to deal with what he has done, my sister is not allowed to have kids. I wasn't even allowed to stay with her when my mom was in the hospital and now I can't get married."

Dan said this as calmly as he could, although you could hear bits of anger come out in his voice. By the time that lunch was over, Dan had me thinking, not only about him, but Elizabeth as well. I was really hoping that tomorrow is going to work out the way that it is supposed to. Because if we fail, then not only do we fail ourselves but we also fail every generation after us. Also, the security in the Dome will increase and I fear the people will lose what little freedom that they have left. Because the Government will make sure that it never happens again.

Mr. Johns' class was rather boring from the start. "Okay class, today's class work and homework will be a ten page report on the President's speech this morning" he said. "Wait no, wait say that again!" I thought to myself, a ten page report on a speech that I really didn't pay attention to it in the first place. How could I even write a report on it! I'm glad that the speech will be aired later on tonight on television. I dreaded that I had to pay attention to that. I sat there drawing little circles on my paper hoping that Mr. Johns didn't want to come over to my desk to see what I was doing. I would have to come up with an excuse on why I wasn't writing. Even if I had paid attention to the speech what would I write about? How wrong it is for the Government to control everybody's lives, or how insane it is for them to tell people who they can marry or not. The fact that a person is told that they can have kids or not, my report itself would be on what's wrong with his country and how it steals from every one. The one thing that they were once granted at birth. I would get an automatic "F" if I did the report that way.

I jumped out of my seat when the school bell rang for the last time that day. I met Elizabeth and Dan at the court after school, we all sat at the bleachers. "Do you think tomorrow is going to work?" Elizabeth asked, "Of course it will! It has too" Dan said. You could hear the uncertainty in his voice, maybe he was doubtful as I was. He was more than likely scared than I was. Now since the President made that speech this morning, Dan had a lot more on the line than I did if this didn't work. "I need your help tonight man" Dan said. I wondered what Dan would need my help for, the action wasn't until tomorrow. Unless he was in on something that I had no idea about. "I don't know if mom will let me go out tonight" I said, "Well think of something!" Dan said in anger.

I'm sure that I could think of something, if I tried hard enough or I couldn't even bother asking Mom and Dad. But if all else fails, I would have to sneak out. It would be risky, but I would have to do it. We all walked to the Cafeteria, we decided that we would sit at the table by ourselves and not with any family members. I thought that it was a good idea from the start. I could make a really good reason why I wanted to spend the night over Dan's again. After dinner, I walked Elizabeth home. At her door she kissed me goodnight, "Tomorrow?" she asked, "Tomorrow" I answered.

As I walked home, I came to realize that today was the strangest day of my life, it had been to quiet and I really didn't like it either. Silence bothers me even at my finest of times. I couldn't even stand it when I am trying to go to sleep. I would lay in bed humming myself to sleep. It was either the speech from this morning or the fact that we are all preparing ourselves for tomorrow. I know that it is going to be pretty crazy, and I really don't know what to expect. But it will be glorious. As I walked thru my front door. I found Dad watching television while Mom was sleeping. "Hey Dad, can I stay over Dan's?" I asked.

"Well, didn't you stay the night over there last night?"

"Yea, but we have a project to work on."

"What kind of project?"

"A ten page report on the speech from this morning."

"Yea, I don't care. I believe Mom washed some of your uniforms today."

"Well that was easy!" I thought to myself. I didn't have to go into detail that much on why I wanted to go. Usually Dad let me do whatever. It was Mom who worried the most. I packed one of my uniforms and my black hoodie, that's all I really needed. I couldn't imagine that I would need anything else. I left my dirty uniform shirt on my floor. I didn't even think about putting it in the dirty cloths bin. In fact my head was a total mess, by this time tomorrow I am going to be free.

As soon as I got to Dan's front door, he opened it before I could even knock. "We need to go now!" Dan said, as he closed the door behind him. "I thought that we were going later?" I asked, "No, now!" he answered. As we walked out of the building, I thought to myself "Why are we leaving now?" The very thought of me carrying my bag out in the open made me nervous, and I was waiting for a cop to stop me. To ask me what I was doing, plus the hoodie that I was wearing was just screaming for attention. When we got to the building, Dan didn't even knock, he just opened the door and walked right in.

The room wasn't like the way that I had seen it before, instead of the rows of chairs, there were four or five tables with people working at them, "You kids get out of here!" a guy yelled at us. Dan just shrugged him off and ignored him. "You kids are not supposed to be in here, get out!" the guy yelled again, "My sister told me to be here!" Dan yelled. "Who is your sister?" the guy asked, "Katherine" Dan answered. The guy's face went completely blank, he looked at me and Dan like he insulted the king himself, and he was waiting to be sent to the gavels, to be hung by the neck.

I didn't know that Katherine had that much power over people, and that Dan knew how to use it. We walked towards the stage where Katherine was sitting, "Well hello boys" she smiled. I smiled back, Dan just sat down right next to her. "What are they doing?" I asked, "They are building the explosives" Katherine answered. "They are making them to look like the control boxes that are on the walls, so that way it won't look weird and the plan would not be exposed." It made sense why they were making them look like the control boxes, which were against the walls. Because if the explosives were just out in the open, they were going to be taken down. If anyone saw them.

"Okay boys, this is what you have to do" Katherine said, "When they are done, you two are going to get three each. You have to place them half way between the real control boxes and they have to be screwed onto the walls. You will also have a fake wire tube that you have to connect from the box into the ground, to make them look as real as possible." Katherine handed both of us a screwdriver, "The screws should be able to get through the wall okay. Just please remember, not to drop them because they will go off and not only will you die. Your mission will be a failure" Katherine said. "After you are done, come back here. Both of you have two hours." Two hours? I wouldn't think that it would be enough time to do all that work. Dan and I got handed the backpacks that contained the explosives. "Screws are in the pockets" Katherine said, as we were walking towards the door. Katherine stopped us, "Wait these are for you." Katherine handed us each a black mask to cover our faces. "These will only cover form the bridge of the nose and down, please be safe!" she said. We put our masks on and headed out the door.

CHAPTER NINE

Dan and I walked our way towards the nearest wall of the Dome, "Why are we doing this?" I asked. "Because I know how to sneak around this place, and Katherine trusts me" Dan answered. I understood why Katherine trusted Dan, I mean he is her little brother. But I mean, we are only kids and to be trusted with such a mission is beyond insane. If I was in her shoes, I wouldn't trust a kid with this kind of mission even one as important as the one that we are doing.

Dan had suddenly stopped, "Shh." he whispered. Then he pointed at the Police Officer that was walking by the opening of the alley way that we were in. My heart began to race as we stood there like a deer in headlights. I had to count to ten to slow down my breathing. The Cop was in our way, we had to cross the street to get into the next alley. That was the last alley that we had to walk in before we got to the wall. Dan had motioned us to go forward, before even going into the street. He poked his head out, to see where the Cop was.

When Dan noticed that the Cop wasn't anywhere in his sight, he put up his hand and counted to three with his fingers. "Run!" he whispered, and we did. We ran like there was no tomorrow or better yet, the mouse that is being chase by the cat. As we walked in the last alley, I started getting doubts "Dan, I don't know if I can do this" I said. "Are you scared?" he asked, "Very" I answered. "Instead of thinking about the mission, think about your future. Maybe with Elizabeth" Dan said. "Only you can find a rose in a bush full of thorns" I laughed. When we reached the end of the alley, we were finally at the wall. I had never seen it up so close before, it was huge! I felt like an ant compared to a giant, "You take that side and I will take this one" Dan said. I agreed, as I walked up to the wall, I began to study the first control box that was in front of me. I looked back at the buildings that were behind me, they were at least a mile back and there was a small garden between the wall and the buildings. I also looked for cops. I am deathly afraid of getting caught.

I walked to the next control box, trying to figure out the halfway point between the boxes. "So…these control everything?" I thought to myself. When I figured out the halfway point, I gently put the backpack on the ground, unzipped it and pulled out one of the fake control boxes. I was extremely happy that the real control boxes were my height, so placing them would be relatively easy. There were four notches on the box, one for each side. I grabbed four screws and put them in the pocket of my hoodie. I took a deep breath, before I grabbed the screwdriver out of my back pocket. I began to screw the box to the wall. I had to use all the force that I had to get one screw into the wall. It would have been a lot easier if I had a drill. It was a lot harder than what Katherine told me, it was going to be.

After I got the box on the wall, I pulled out one of the cords from the backpack. It had two brackets, one at the top and one on the bottom to hold it in place against the wall. I got four more screws from the backpack. I lined the cord to the box as perfectly as possible. "One down, two more to go" I thought to myself. I did the other two as I did the first box, as gently and as perfect as I possibly could. I was tired after everything that I had done. I couldn't even believe that I had done it in the first place. I would have been sent to jail for the rest of my life, if I had gotten caught.

I waited in the alley for Dan to get done, which was very shortly after I did. "Let's go, we only have a half hour left" Dan said, "A half hour until what?" I asked. "A half hour until the cameras get turned back on" He answered, "Oh" I said. We rushed our way back to the building, we checked for cops along the way. When we got down to the basement, the only person that was there was Katherine. She was waiting for us to return safely, "Done?" she asked. "Done!" Dan answered, and then he curled up on the stage and fell asleep. "Katherine, what is going to happen to the Government after tomorrow?" I asked, "It will shut down because it has failed to do its purpose" she answered.

"And what is that?"

"The entire reason the Government was created, was to protect a free nation. But since we are not free, the Dome's system was created to rule and put fear over its people."

"Why was the Dome created?"

"No one knows Zack, they tell us over and over again that we have destroyed the land out there. But I believe it was created to control the people completely."

"Do you think this will ever happen again?"
"Not anytime in our future, at least we won't see it. But if people scream for a better Government along with justice for the injustice

that is in that system, then yes, this will happen again. Zack we lead by example. Don't fret, when people are doing things you don't agree with. Instead look upon the leaders that they have followed and the examples that they have set."

Katherine was right on point. "Go to sleep, you have had a big day today and you will have a bigger day tomorrow" she said. She walked out of the room. As I laid my head on the stage. I fell asleep only to be woken up by the alarm on my watch going off. "Dan, wake up its time to go" I said while shaking him to wake up. I got my uniform on like any other normal day, Dan already had his uniform on. We walked to the Cafeteria, and we ate breakfast. Well I tried, my stomach was in knots by that point and there was no sign of it getting any better. I kept on saying "You're okay" in my head, but that wasn't helping at all, "Are you okay man?" Dan asked "You look like you're going to be sick." I looked at him, "Yea, I am okay" truth was, I was really going to be sick, and my mind was racing at a thousand miles per hour.

After breakfast, we walked to school. I began to think of ways to distract the class enough for the cops to be called. Since Katherine had told me nine on the dot, that would not be a problem. Considering my class at that time would be Mr. Smith's, he was rather easy to get in a twisted bind. During Mrs. Keen's class, I couldn't even think at all about class work. Neither could Mrs. Keen, she was still upset about yesterday. You could tell that she still was, just by the assignment that she gave us. And that was just to read. That was it, no questions, just reading. I sat there pretending that I was reading, when I looked up at the clock it was eight thirty. Class gets out in fifteen minutes, and Mr. Smith's class started ten minutes after that.

My stomach began to turn even more, I walked up to Mrs. Keen and asked her if I could go into the bathroom. I tried my best not to run to the bathroom, because if I ran. I would get caught by a hall monitor and if I got caught. I would puke all over the floor, than they would have no choice but to send me home. And I didn't want that to happen. As soon as I walked into the bathroom. I had to run to the nearest stall, I ended up bowing down to the porcelain gods. Losing everything that was in my stomach until there was nothing left. "That's it Zack, pull yourself together!" I thought to myself, that is exactly what I did too. I slugged my way to one of the sinks, washed my face, and looked in the mirror. I stood up tall like I was presenting myself to a noble crowd, I tugged on my uniform jacked. I took a deep breath and gave myself the meanest look that I could ever give myself.

On my walk back to class, I thought of a way to get the class in a roar. "I'll take a softball from the gym" I said to myself. Considering the storage room is never locked, and 99% of the time. Mr. Clyde was in his office when the bell rang. That gives me enough time to take a ball and run. The bell rang as soon as I got back into Mrs. Keen's classroom. I quickly grabbed my things from my seat, then I quickly made my way to the gym. I peaked my head in the gym looking for Mr. Clyde, but he was nowhere to be found. I snuck into the storage room and grabbed a softball. It was one of those big squishy ones, so that way if it hit anyone. It wouldn't hurt them, and I stuffed it in my bag.

When I got to Mr. Smith's class, it was 8:53. I had seven minutes until I had to create chaos. Mr. Smith had the normal problems on the board, I started doing them in my notebook trying to act as normal as I possibly could. I just kept looking at the clock, the time kept on going slower and slower. Minutes seemed like hours, and seconds seemed like years. When nine o'clock had hit, I looked over at Adrian. "Hey, you want to play ball?" I asked, "Not now I am trying to focus!" he growled. Then I thought of one person that would not turn me down at all. That was Jay, he was across the room and he would not deny any chance to get out of class work. I wouldn't blame him at all either, I grabbed my bag acting like I was getting something out of it. I placed my hand firmly on the ball, and got it out of my bag.

"Hey Jay, catch!" I yelled, Jay looked up at me as I threw the ball at him. "Let's play around the room" I laughed, Jay smiled up at me as he started tossing the ball around the room. Mr. Smith started banging his ruler on his desk, "Boys stop it!" he yelled. The class ignored him, he stormed out of the classroom. Straight down to Mr. Anderson's officer. The class kept on tossing the ball around. They were having way too much fun. It's been way too long since we have had any fun in the class, everything has been so boring and no one could even stand it. I was having fun as well.

Mr. Anderson came storming into the classroom, "Everyone stop it!" he yelled. "No!" I yelled back, if that wasn't a cue to call the police, I don't know what is. "Everyone stop it right now!" he yelled, no one would listen. The only one who wasn't taking part of the fun was Adrian, he was trying way too hard to focus on his school work. Eventually he broke focus to join in, I got up from my chair and walked towards the door. "Where do you think you're going?" Mr. Anderson asked, "None of your business!" I answered. I was really going down to Dan's classroom to invite him in. Mr. Anderson knew what was really going on, so he let me walk on by. Dan was a couple of classrooms down and when I got to his room. I pushed the door open so hard that it bounced off the wall. The loud noise that it made got everybody's attention. "We are playing ball, come on let's go!" I yelled. "Let's go!" Dan laughed. Soon enough both mine and Dan's classrooms were in the hallway playing with the ball.

Dan started to go to every classroom, getting everyone to join in the fun that was going on in the hallway. Every teacher tried to get everyone to stop, even the hall monitors couldn't stop them. But no one would listen. In all the chaos I found Elizabeth laughing, "Is this because of you?" she asked. "I had to think of something" I answered, it worked. I created chaos, some of the students didn't even bother playing with the rest of the other students. They began to rip paper and posters off of the walls. "The cops have been called, this is your last chance!" yelled Mr. Anderson, "No one listen to him! They can't do anything!" Dan yelled, some of the skittish students went right back into their classrooms in fear of getting caught by the police. They didn't want to get in trouble or worst yet, get sent to jail. They didn't know what was really happening, they wouldn't cower in fear if they really knew.

The cops had come to a school that was in full and utter chaos, they were amazed that the school couldn't handle the student body. In fact the cops were even puzzled on how to solve such a mess, since it's been years since they had to deal with something like this. They had no idea on what to do, one of the cops had a megaphone "Everyone please stop it and go back to your class. We don't want to have to take action" he said. "Take action?" I thought to myself, what would they do? I heard over one of the cop's radios that a protest had broken out at one of the zones and that they needed help. Then another cop called in asking for help at a neighboring school. There was something going on in at least every zone, the police had their handful. They acted like they were in quicksand and they didn't know how to get out.

All of a sudden there was a loud bang that echoed in everyone's ears, then one loud bang after another. Everyone in the hallway stopped to listen, to hear what was going on. One of the cop's radios was loud enough for everyone to hear it, "There has been multiple explosions, we need help!" the person screamed over the radio. All of the cops rushed outside, all of the students, teachers, and the rest of the faculty followed behind them. All you could see was the holes in the dome wall. Every single person stood outside with their mouths wide open.

"We did it!" I said to myself, no one could believe it. There were huge holes in the wall, "What's going on?" Mrs. Keen asked. "Your freedom!" I answered, she just stood there for a minute. "I've got to go home and pack!" she laughed, Mrs. Keen started crying again. But this time she wasn't sad, those were tears of happiness. Mrs. Keen wasn't the only one who was crying, Elizabeth was too. "Elizabeth go home pack, and get your Grandpa ready. I'll meet you at your house as soon as possible" I told her.

Without even saying a word or even thinking, she ran to her building. The rest of the people were still standing there with their mouths wide open, "What is everybody doing? Go home! Get your things and let's get out of here!" I yelled. Suddenly everyone went into a panic, running to their homes as fast as they could. I ran home as fast as I could, dodging other people running. When I got home, I found Mom staring out of the living room window, while Dad was flipping through television channels. Trying to see what was going on, "Zack, what's happening?" Dad asked. "Someone blew holes in the wall, get up and get things packed. Let's go!" I answered. Dad instantly got up from the couch, ran into the bedroom and packed whatever he could. Mom on the other hand stood there still looking out of the window, "They won't let us free, you know that as much as I do!" she said.

How could she think like that? I just don't get it. She has a chance to be free and she is not going to take it, maybe she is too scared to even think about freedom. Mom is used to this kind of life style that the slightest bit of change made her tuck in her tail between her legs like scared dog. "Come on Emmie! Take this chance, this is the one thing that you will regret not doing!" Dad yelled, "But Al! You know as well as I do, they will not let us out!"

Mom yelled back. "It's worth a chance! I am taking it with or without you!" Dad said, I believe that what Dad said was her wakeup call, because she got her bag and put whatever she could in it.

I went into my room and grabbed my other bag, since I left mine at school. Dusted it off and packed all the clothes that I had. I left my school uniforms behind, since I didn't need them anymore. After I packed, I started to walk out the door. "Where are you going?" Dad asked, "To help Elizabeth, she needs to get her Grandpa out of here" I answered. As I walked out the door, there was no chance of my parents stopping me what so ever. This was something that I promised myself that I was going to do. No one was going to stop me.

I'd never seen so many people on the streets in my entire life, people carried whatever they could. Either in their bags, or they had a bundle of things in their hands. I ran to Elizabeth's building. It was extremely hard to get in since there was an endless crowd pouring out of the main doors. The inside was no better either, since people were crowding the stairs and elevator like there was no tomorrow. It felt like a complete waste of time trying to get up the stairs, even though it wasn't.

When I got to Elizabeth's door, I was completely out of breath and I was tired. I didn't even bother knocking either, I just walked right in. "Hi there Zacky boy!" John smiled, "You ready?" I asked. "Ready for what?" John asked. "To be free!" I laughed, John looked at me confused then he yelled for Elizabeth. "Yes?" she asked, "Get my things!" John yelled. "I'm already working on it" Elizabeth said. She walked back into his room, to finish packing his things. When she was done, she came out with two duffle bags that looked like they were filled to the point that they could burst. "Zack, Grandpa is going to need help walking. His back is hurting him." "I don't need any help!" John yelled. John put both of his hands firmly on the armrests of his chair, slowly he lifted himself up. When he got his hands off of the armrests, he fell back into the chair. "Okay, I need help" he said "You okay with the bags?" I asked Elizabeth. "Yea" she answered, I walked over to John. He looked like he was in a lot of pain, "Are you okay?" I asked.

"Yes, I'll be fine" he answered, "Give me your hand" I told him. When he reached out towards me, I grabbed his hand and knelt down. I put his arm around the back of my neck, "Okay on the count of three, One…Two…Three!" I said. At the end of three. I used all my strength to lift him up, there was a lot of weight, just on my shoulders alone. I don't know if he was trying to help me get him up, or his back is really hurting him that bad. I looked at it like this was his only chance to get his freedom back, and I was going to help him get it. Even if it meant that I had to break my own back, trying to help him.

We had to take baby steps to get John to start walking, stopping only when he asked. We were halfway to the stairs, when John had asked to rest against the wall. "I cannot go any further, unless I rest" he said. I agreed with him as I walked towards the nearest wall, I needed to rest too. John is bigger than me and trying to carry him alone was a task within itself. "John we need to go" I said, "Okay" he whispered. We started down the steps, taking one step at a time until we had reached the bottom. While we were walking down the steps, people didn't have the decency to wait for him to reach the bottom. They either shoved Elizabeth to the side, or complained that we were taking too long. I was relieved when we have reached the bottom.

The madness didn't really start until we had reached the outside. Crowds of people were still making their way to the holes in the dome walls. Getting past the crowd was extremely hard, since other people were moving at a thousand miles per hour just to get out and I was moving about five or ten tops. When we got closer to one of the holes in the wall, there was an even bigger crowd and it wasn't going anywhere.

CHAPTER TEN

"What's going on?" I asked "Cops are there, they won't let anyone out" a woman answered. First thing that I had thought to myself was that Mom was right, they won't let anyone free. "John, do you think that you could make it up front?" I asked. "Yes I can, not even death can stop us now boy-o!" he laughed, I looked over at Elizabeth "Let's go!" she said. We had started making our way to the front of the crowd, people were packed together like sardines in a can. "What do you think that you are doing?" a voice said. I turned around only to find out that Dan was behind me, "Trying to be free" I said. Dan walked to the other side of John and put John's other arm on his shoulders. "You look like you need help" Dan laughed, "We are in this together" I said. "We started this, we have to finish it!" Dan yelled. Me, Dan, John, and Elizabeth walked right up to the front. You could hear the people screaming at the cops to let them go, but the cops wouldn't budge at all.

There were four cops at each hole, holding back the crowds from getting out. "We are ordered to keep you in this Dome, no matter the cost" The Cop said, "The system has broken you have to let us go" I said. "No, the system is still in full force as long as you the people remain in this Dome!" the Cop said. Katherine didn't say anything about this, I thought that if the holes were created in the walls, that the system would break. I didn't think the system would remain as long as the people remained within the Dome. "So, you're telling me, that if even one person leaves the Dome right now, that the system would break?" Dan asked. "Yes" answered the Cop.

Dan looked at me, "You thinking what I'm thinking?" he asked. "Don't do it!" I laughed, Dan had taken John's arm off of his shoulders, braced himself than punched the Cop right in the face. The other cops were dumbfounded, they had never dealt with violence from a citizen against a cop before. They stepped aside when the crowd started rushing their way out the hole towards the outside. "Dan, right?" John asked, "Yes sir" Dan answered. "That was a mighty fine thing of you to do" John laughed. "Thank you" Dan said, Dan was shaking John's hand. Then he put John's arm back on his shoulders, very slowly. We had made our way outside, I couldn't believe my eyes at what I was seeing. I had to do a double take, the outside was not like the outside that the Government had been telling us over the years.

There was nothing dead or deformed. There were trees that looked like they could go on for miles. The grass was so green that it even put a leprechaun to shame. The only things that looked like it was destroyed were the buildings that we had left behind. Mother Nature had taken over them, even the roads were destroyed and had new life growing out of the cracks. New smells had my nose going crazy, along with the sensation of the warmth of the sun that touched my skin. I was hearing real birds for the first time in my life. "Are we in heaven?" John asked, "No but it seems like it!" I laughed. "I thought I would die before seeing this again" he said. "Well that didn't happen" Dan smiled.

Everyone was in a complete shock that they were seeing the same thing that I was. I wasn't the only one that realized at that moment that the Government was lying to us the entire time. It made me think about the other things that they possibly lied to us about. I didn't want to ruin this beautiful moment by angry thoughts. I began to watch little kids play in the grass, rolling down the nearest hills. Little girls picking up the beautiful flowers that laid around them. It was like they had an instinct to know what all this was even though it was all new to them, as it was to me. "Is this what it is like?" I asked, "This is exactly what it is like" she answered.

All John wanted to do was sit in the grass, and feel the warmth of the sun on him. I didn't blame him one bit, Elizabeth took my hand. She made me run with her and led me under a tree. It was big and it had pink flowers that dangled from the branches. Elizabeth had told me that it was a cherry blossom tree and that she had only seen one when she went on vacation to Japan with her parents. "Wait? You've been to Japan?" I asked, "Yea, and all over Europe too" she answered. "Well you learn something new every day, I guess" I muttered. Elizabeth laughed at me. I felt embarrassed because that was really a stupid remark but I am glad that she got amusement out of it.

We laid there underneath the tree for a little bit, Elizabeth rolled onto her stomach.

"What do you think is going to happen now Zack?"

"I don't know."

"Well what you do want to happen?"

"I don't want the future generations to suffer like ours did. And the generations before us suffered more than we did, because they had their freedom stolen away from them."

"Why do you think the Government did this to the American people?"

"That I don't know, I don't think that anyone knows besides the people who had done it. I mean, the President was just a pawn in the game that they called a system. The Government gained the control over the people because they lied and put fear in the people, if you put enough fear in someone then you can control them like a puppet and you can get that person to do whatever you want."

"Lies and fear is all it takes, Zack you put it into terms that are in its purest form."

I just laughed, "I should write about our victory" I said. Elizabeth laughed harder than I did. "I want to go swimming" Elizabeth said. "Swimming?" I asked, "Yes!" she answered. I have not ever went swimming unless you count being in the bathtub when I was little. "The Ocean is not too far from here, I remember seeing it when I was coming here" she said. The Ocean? I haven't seen one besides in the books that I would read at school. You could catch a glimpse of a picture of one in a history textbook only if a battle had happened at one during a war. I didn't know that the Ocean was even near the dome in the first place, and I was more than happy to go.

Elizabeth and I started walking, the Ocean was about two miles from where the Dome was. I couldn't believe it either, the Ocean of all things! Neighboring the Dome and no one knew about it, and even if they did, they never said a word about it, it was beautiful. The pictures that I had seen couldn't compare to the real thing at all. Elizabeth was not the only one that had the idea about going to the Ocean. People were on the beach sitting in the sand talking to each other, while other people were in the water playing around.

I started thinking about what other people were seeing for the first time, what they couldn't believe that they were missing out on during this entire time. The Dome itself is huge and people were looking at other things while I was looking at this. I'm still wondering on how Elizabeth knew that the Ocean was so close to the part of the Dome that we lived at. "Take off your shoes! You're free! You can do what you want now" Elizabeth laughed, she was right and that is exactly what I did. I took off my shoes and my socks, as I walked on the sand with my bare feet. I could only think about how weird it felt against my skin, if the heat from the sand didn't melt the skin off of the bottom of my feet first.

Elizabeth took off her shoes too, she began laughing as she jumped and twirled around in the air. She was like a kid again, "Come on!" she giggled while she grabbed my hand. She dragged me into the water, "Why does it have to be so cold!" I shouted. "Because it's the Ocean!" Elizabeth shouted back, "You will get used to it" she said. I don't know if I could ever get used to this, my showers are not even this cold. I was dying to get back on the warm beach. I played in the water with Elizabeth until I couldn't handle the cold anymore, plus my clothes being soaked with the old water wasn't something that I really wanted.

"I'm going back on the beach, where it is warm!" I said. Elizabeth decided to stay in the water going further and further while I watched her on the beach getting dry and warm. Eventually she came back onto the beach to sit down and join me, "Zack?" she asked. I looked over at her and she surprised me with a kiss. "I love you!" she said, I have got to admit. I wasn't expecting that at all. I was waiting for her to ask me a question, not a kiss. "I love you too!" I said. We sat at the beach until the sun went down over the water. I wrote that moment down in my head so I could have it forever. When we got back near the Dome, there was a huge party going on. More like a festival, people were having fun for the first time in their lives. "Food is over there and guess what! It doesn't taste like garbage!" Dan said as he walked up to us.

There were tables upon tables of food, all of it looked good and smelled beyond good. Louie was tending to the tables while cooking the food on a huge fire. "Eat up guys, enjoy your first night of freedom!" He said, he handed both me and Elizabeth plates. I piled mine with food, from hot dogs to hamburgers. I also had some fried potatoes and corn on the cob, my heart sank when I took the first bite. I had never tasted food this good before, I was used to the garbage that they served in the Cafeteria. After me and Elizabeth got done eating, which was rather quickly because we were both shoveling the food down our throats. We just sat and watched people danced around while some of the other people sang songs that they could remember. This entire thing was completely new to me, freedom was no longer just a word of a forgotten dream anymore. It was a reality, John found the spot that me and Elizabeth were sitting at. "You know, I always thought freedom was a distant reality since the Dome was created" he said, "I never thought in my wildest dreams that I would see freedom ever again."

"Well Grandpa, you are now going to be free for the rest of your life."

"Your parents are as proud of you as I am Lizzy."

John hugged Elizabeth and gave her a kiss on her forehead, in the corner of my eye I could see that Katherine was walking up to us with Dan. "Enjoying yourselves?" she asked, "Very!" I answered.

"Thank you Zack, if it wasn't for you and Dan, we wouldn't be here right now."

"It was you that came up with the plan, Dan nor myself can't take all of the credit. I mean we all had a hand in this."

"I know, but it was you and Dan who planted the boxes."

"So what is going to happen now Katherine?"

"Well the system is shut down since there is no one besides some Government Officials left in the Dome. We as a people are going to have to rebuild the system, people have the rights that they used to have before the Dome. We are also going to inhabit these buildings after rebuilding them or touching them up. I mean we don't want to step foot in the Dome again and the people need a place to live. Eventually, the dome is going to be destroyed along with everything that it holds within it. This is our fresh start Zack, and it's time that we take total advantage of it. We also need to ensure that this will never happen again."

I wondered about the process and the steps that needed to be taken to rebuild the Government that fits the American people along with the points that they would be happy with. There would have to be a lot of thinking that would have to be involved. Also to get the people out of the puppet mind state, that would be hard enough. Even though some people have already did it, while others are just riding along waiting to be put back in the cage that they called home for so long. You could tell by the crowd, at first they wanted their freedom than they had second thoughts about it. Doubting themselves and what they had done.

The faces of the doubters were blank and emotionless. I don't think that this reality of freedom has hit them yet, like it did others. They remained as scared as they were in the Dome, "So you had a hand in this?" John asked. "Yes I did" I answered, "Thank you" he said while shaking my hand. "Your kids, grandkids, and future generations are going to be talking about you for years and years to come". I don't think that I am that important in all of this, I just did my part and craved my freedom enough to get it. I was just doing what I was told, I mean that was nothing new. I did whatever I was told to do every day, what makes this so special? I felt a little bit different because of everything that I was seeing and the things that I had come to realize. Not by my actions, but I guess what I have done is something that would go down in the history books for the future generations to read. I should be proud of it too.

In the distance you could see Katherine get on one of the tables that Louie had cleared. "Please everyone, can I have your attention" she said, everybody stopped what they were doing to look up at her. She was speaking as loud as she could to get everyone's attention, at least everyone that could hear her. "My name is Katherine, I used to work for the Government. I interviewed people at the Police Stations, watched the cameras, a lot of you, I know by your name. Most of you I only know by your face, where you lived, or where you worked. I was one of the top Government Officials and some of the things that I have done, I am not proud of but I had no choice but to do them. I worked for the Government because I wanted to know how it worked on the inside. I was disgusted with what I had seen, and a lot I wish I could erase from my memory" she paused. "Some of you know that I held meetings in a basement late at night, the holes were not created at random. They were planned, those were not the only holes created in the Dome either. They were created everywhere, everybody that lived in that Dome is now free. I could understand that this is a huge change for a lot of you, I can ensure you that you are not going back in that Dome. When we left that place as a group of people, the Government system had shut itself down due to the Failure Act. If the Government fails its main purpose it has no choice but to shut down, and we shut it down! Now we as Americans have to start with a new Government system that actually stands true to its word, and that is for the people by the people. Myself a long with the Government officials that I had personally worked with, will work on a Government system that the people can agree with. I can also say this, that the Constitution is no longer just a piece of paper anymore, it is now a guideline that the Government must and will follow and enforce. I would also like to take a minute to thank the people that helped make this happen, without you guys this wouldn't have happened. Now do you guys have any questions?"

Hands started going up rapidly, I don't think Katherine was ready for so many people to ask questions. "What about the prisoners that the Government kept locked up over the years?" a woman asked, "Since the system is shut down, they have to be released. If they are not already, they will be by tomorrow morning" Katherine answered. "What are we going to do for food?" a man asked, "Farmers have agreed to keep the farms up and running for the meantime until they find new land to inhabit. Don't worry all the basics have been covered" she answered,

Katherine kept on answering questions for a while, I started questioning myself on where were my parents. I got up from where I was sitting, told Elizabeth that I needed to find them and I went off searching for them. It took me a while to find them, but eventually I found them sitting on the beach looking up at the stars. Dad was holding Mom in his arms, "Oh, how romantic!" I laughed. They both looked up at me, "Hey Zack!" Dad said "We are free!" Mom giggled. "You know Zack, right now I feel like a teenager again, when I first took Mom on a date" Dad said.

It was good to hear Dad say that since the Dome was created, he was put to work as soon as we got in. He built the cameras that people had inside their homes, he really never had the time for himself or Mom. It was a good thing that he finally had it, I wasn't going to spoil their moment any more than I already had. I walked away from them to find my own spot on the beach, I took off my uniform jacket. During the chaos, I didn't even think about changing clothes, I took my jacket, folded it up, and placed it behind my head. I looked up at the stars. I had learned about them in school, but I really never got the chance to see them since curfew. You really couldn't see them thru the glass roof of the dome. It was truly remarkable.

I started thinking about the possibilities that laid ahead and how we could learn from the mistakes that we had made as a people to make a better future. That was really the point in the first place, was to learn on what to do and what not to do. I wondered how glorious the future would be, I got in one of my deep thought states that I couldn't hear anything that was going on around me. I couldn't even hear Elizabeth talking to me, "Zack" she yelled. "Yes?" I asked, "I asked if I could join you!" she said. "Sure" I laughed, she looked at me like I was stupid. She probably thought that I was an idiot for laughing at her. Elizabeth laid her head on my chest. She was listening to my heartbeat, I didn't understand it but I wasn't going to question it as long as she was with me. "What are you doing?" she asked, "Looking at the stars" I answered.

Elizabeth started talking about the possibilities of other creatures out there in other galaxies looking down at us. Shaking their heads while calling the human race idiots. It was all nonsense the way that she was talking. I couldn't imagine other creatures in the universe looking down at us. From what I had learned in school, Earth is the only planet that has life on it. Even though that could be another lie that the Government had told us, and put it in school textbooks to make it seem real and reasonable. There could be that possibility after all, we would never know and honestly, I didn't care about finding out either way.

After a while, Elizabeth folded her jacked like mine and laid next to me. We both watched the stars, we were even lucky enough to see a couple of shooting stars go across the sky. Elizabeth fell asleep, while I laid there wide awake. Thoughts kept on going off in my head, the same thought kept coming back. "I'm free!" I said to myself, it really wasn't sinking in until now. I kept on pinching myself expecting to wake up from a dream. One thing I sure was happy about, is that everything that had happened in my dream from the other night. It didn't happen. Katherine was right about that part, besides Dan punching a cop. But he had a reason too, he wanted to be free. I got excited at the very thought of never going to the Dome ever again, I smiled in complete and utter joy.

My name is Zack Helenkopf, I am no longer number 578648548. I am a part of the generation that freed America and the American people. I am free.

Made in the USA
Middletown, DE
07 September 2021

47697941R00076